The
Usborne Book
of
Greek
Myths

Anna Milbourne and Louie Stowell

Illustrated by Simona Bursi,
Elena Temporin and Petra Brown

Edited by Ruth Brocklehurst and Gill Doherty
Designed by Nicola Butler
Consultant: James Brown

Contents

The myths

Thousands of years ago, the Ancient Greeks told each other stories of gods, monsters, heroes and heroines. The myths have been passed down to us through the generations, but the tales they tell go back to the very beginning of time itself...

The birth
of the
gods

At first, according to the Ancient Greeks, there were no gods or people, no day or night, no planets or stars. There was just nothingness that stretched on and on forever. Then, out of nowhere, the earth appeared. She was beautiful, with a curved shape and a warm heart.

A split second later, the sky came into being. He was everything she was not. While the earth was calm and steady-going, with hidden depths, the sky was quick and changeable, and couldn't hide anything if he tried.

The sky loved the earth so much that he wrapped himself around her and swore they would never be parted. And, at first, she felt the same way.

The earth's name was Gaia, and the sky was called Uranus. When she first kissed him, he blazed red and gold, making the very first sunset. When Uranus bent his star-crowned head to sleep beside Gaia, he bathed her hills and valleys in silver light.

Very soon they decided to start a family. They were so vast themselves that all of their children turned out to be immense too. First came the titans: a race of giants and giantesses so huge that they could pluck trees as if they were daisies, and sit on the mountains as if they were thrones. They were beautiful and strong, and their parents were very proud.

Next, Gaia gave birth to three cyclops: stout, ugly giants who each had just one large, bulging eye. Gaia thought they were perfect, but Uranus wasn't so sure. "They're not as good-looking as their brothers and sisters," he remarked flatly.

Their next three children were even more monstrous. Each of them had fifty heads and a hundred hands. If their mother was any less pleased with them than with her other children, she didn't show it. But their father couldn't bear the sight of them. "They're hideous!" he exclaimed when he saw them. "Can't they live underground – and their ugly cyclops brothers too? They're spoiling my view." And he pushed them back inside the earth.

Gaia was heartbroken, and wept rivers of tears at Uranus's cruelty. He was miserable at having upset her. His tears fell as rain and mingled with hers, streaming down hills and pooling in valleys to form great, salty seas.

But, however much he regretted hurting Gaia, Uranus couldn't hide how he felt. "I still love you," he told her. "But I can't love them." Gaia grew more and more resentful. Secretly, she began to plan a way to get rid of Uranus and set her imprisoned children free.

One day she said to the titans, "Your father is old.
He is growing weaker by the day. One of you must rule
next, and the time has come for you to take control."

Despite their great size, the titans all trembled
at the thought of challenging their father.
All except one. His name was Cronus.

"I'll do it, Mother," he said. "Just tell me how."

"Climb to the top of the highest mountain,"
she told him, "and I'll show you." Cronus did as she
asked. When he reached the top of the mountain,
a sickle emerged from the rocks in front of him,
its curved blade gleaming in the sun.

"This weapon is made from adamant, the hardest
part of me," his mother told him. "It is the only
thing that can possibly harm your father."

Cronus picked up the sickle, and his
mother called out in a sweet voice.
"Uranus, come here, darling."

Cronus could almost feel the weight
of the sky above him as he waited. Then a
wind blew, the clouds rearranged themselves,
and his father appeared. "I'm here, my love,"
Uranus whispered.

Cronus swung the sickle with all
his might. The blade flashed as it sliced
through the sky.

When Uranus was attacked, drops of his blood fell into the ocean. Moments later, a figure emerged from the foaming waves. She was so beautiful it took your breath away. Her name was Aphrodite and she was the goddess of love.

Uranus's gasp of pain rang out across the universe as he was separated forever from the earth. Cronus knew that he had overthrown his father, and he watched triumphantly as Uranus's face began to fade. "It comes to us all," Uranus said sadly. "One day, you will give way to your own child."

"Never!" cried Cronus, full of the confidence of youth.

He had just set off back down the mountain, when Gaia's voice rang out. "Well done. Now he's gone, you can set your brothers free."

To his mother's dismay, Cronus shook his head. "They'll only get in the way just now," he said. "Maybe I'll do it later."

He asked another titan, Rhea, to marry him, and they decided to start a family. But despite his confidence, Cronus's father's prediction lingered uncomfortably in his mind. When Rhea gave birth to their first child, he swallowed the baby whole, before she even had time to look at it. "What are you doing?" Rhea screamed.

"Calm down, you silly thing," Cronus said. "This is the best way to keep children safe. Didn't you know?"

Rhea shook her head doubtfully. It sounded like a strange idea, but Cronus seemed so certain, and she didn't know any other titans who'd had children, so she supposed it must be normal. Still, she missed the child terribly.

A while later, she gave birth to their second child. Cronus was about to swallow it when Rhea pleaded, "Couldn't we keep the baby here just for a short time?"

Cronus frowned at her. "Don't you want what's best for our family?" he demanded. She nodded sadly, and watched him swallow the second baby whole.

In the following years, their third, fourth and fifth children were dealt with in the very same way.

When Gaia saw what was happening, she was furious with her son. "Your children aren't safe, they are trapped inside your husband," she told Rhea, "just like my children are trapped inside me."

"I knew something wasn't right!" Rhea exclaimed. By this time, she was already pregnant with their sixth child. "I'm not letting him swallow this one," she said, wrapping her arms around her belly.

When it was time for her to have the baby, she went to a cave in the mountains and gave birth in secret. The baby was a boy. Rhea was delighted with him, and named him Zeus.

New life was springing up on the earth all this time. When Rhea's baby was born, Gaia sent a team of gentle creatures called nymphs to help look after him. Leaving the baby in their care, Rhea returned to her husband. She handed him a boulder wrapped in blankets. "Here's our sixth child for you to keep safe," she said innocently, and Cronus swallowed the boulder without suspecting a thing.

The baby Zeus was so powerful that his cries shook the very mountains, but nymphs standing guard outside the cave caught them in soft clouds so that his father wouldn't hear. Those inside the cave comforted him with songs, and fed him on milk and honey.

Nymphs were beautiful, magical girls who never grew old. They came into being along with the trees, rivers, mountains and lakes, and it was their job to take care of nature.

Tree nymphs were known as dryads.

Naiads were water nymphs.

13

Rhea visited her son whenever she could. She told him all about his grandparents, and about what his father had done. Zeus grew up very quickly, and as soon as he was old enough to leave his hiding place, he went to see his father.

"Who are you?" Cronus asked the youth who was glaring at him with a thunderous expression.

Without word of an explanation, Zeus punched Cronus hard in the stomach. "Your time's up, Father," he said. The giant doubled over and out of his gaping mouth sprang the boulder he'd swallowed, followed by five of his children, now fully grown.

Some say Cronus was the same god as Chronos, which means 'time'. Some even say that he still exists, lurking at the edges of the universe, swallowing everything he can lay his hands on. Perhaps it's true. In the end, everything is swallowed up by time.

Together, Zeus and all his brothers and sisters turned to face their father. They were young, powerful and very, very angry. Cronus took one look at their six, glowering faces and knew at once that he was beaten.

Cronus was banished from the face of the earth, and the brothers and sisters set about exploring it. As they went, they discovered that they each had their own amazing powers, that set them above all other beings. Zeus and his siblings were the first gods.

Zeus adored playing with the sky. He loved to shape thunder clouds with his bare hands, and send thunderbolts across the sky in dramatic flashes. When his brother, Poseidon, saw the rolling oceans, he parted the waves with his hands to discover a whole host of startled creatures at the bottom. Their sister, Demeter, found she had green fingers, and spent days coaxing flowers into bloom and trees into fruit.

14

The earth herself, their grandmother Gaia, watched peacefully as they tried out their various powers. "Finally I can go to sleep," she thought, "and trust my family to keep everything safe." But there was one thing she had to take care of first.

"Will you at last set my children free?" she asked Zeus, and she told him about the one-eyed cyclops and their hundred-handed, fifty-headed brothers all imprisoned within her.

"Of course I will," Zeus agreed.

Gaia opened up a gateway so that he could enter the earth and travel deep underground. So along with his two brothers, Poseidon and Hades, Zeus set off to rescue his monstrous uncles.

Deep inside, they discovered a whole different world to the one above. It was lit with an eerie light instead of the sun, and its fields were full of gemstones rather than flowers. "It's wonderful down here," said Hades. "I feel right at home. Let's call it the Underworld."

Even further down, there was a series of warm, pitch-black caverns. Here they found the hundred-handers. Although these monsters were pleased to hear that they were free, they had grown to like living underground. So they decided to stay.

"In that case you can be the guardians of this place," suggested Zeus. "We'll make it a dungeon for those who have done terrible things in their lifetimes." The hundred-handers agreed, and the caverns they guarded came to be known as Tartarus.

The Underworld became the place where the shadowy souls of humans went after they died. It was made up of many different realms. While criminals were sent to Tartarus, heroes and good people entered the beautiful and carefree Elysian Fields.

The gods went on to
have children of their
own – more gods and
goddesses, including:

Athena,
the goddess
of war, who
sprang to life
out of Zeus's head,
fully grown, armed
and dangerous...

Dionysus, the god of
wine, who was born
out of Zeus's thigh...

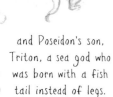

and Poseidon's son,
Triton, a sea god who
was born with a fish
tail instead of legs.

Next, Zeus and his brothers went to find the cyclops. They had made their home in the gleaming seams of metal beneath the mountains, but were terribly squashed and unhappy there. Overjoyed to be set free, they followed the three gods back up to the earth's surface.

Once the rescue was complete, Zeus decided the next thing to be done was to divide up his father's kingdom between his brothers and sisters. He took the heavens for himself, and asked his most beautiful and loyal sister, Hera, to join him. She became the goddess of marriage and faithfulness. Poseidon was given the oceans to rule, and Hades the Underworld. Demeter's role was to tend to all growing things. Their youngest sister, Hestia, didn't want a realm to rule, and so it was agreed she should look after the hearth and home.

The cyclops were so grateful to the gods that they presented them with gifts. Poseidon received a trident to help him control the oceans, Hades was given a cap that made its wearer invisible and Zeus received a shining set of thunderbolts.

After that, the cyclops built a grand palace for the gods. They set it on the clouds above the world's highest mountain, and the gods named it Olympus. Demeter shrouded the top of the mountain in clouds, so that only chosen guests could ever catch a glimpse of the great palace of the gods.

Meanwhile, down below, ordinary men and women were being born and living their lives like tiny ants beneath the gods' powerful gaze...

16

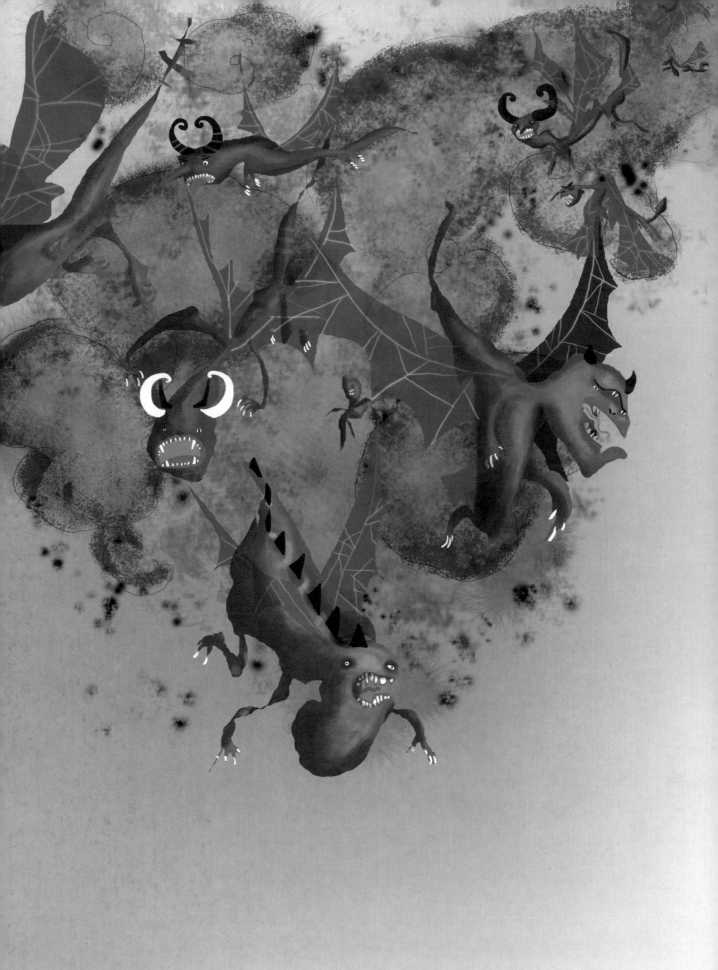

Pandora's box

One morning, Zeus awoke to the delicious smell of freshly baked bread. He'd spent all night at a party with the other gods and was feeling rather tired and grumpy. "Hestia, bring me some of that bread for my breakfast," he shouted, somewhat rudely. His sister was the only one of the gods who ever did any baking.

Hestia's puzzled face appeared around the door. "I don't know who's making bread but it's not me," she said.

"Who else can it be?" grumbled Zeus, getting out of bed. He followed the smell out of the palace to a gap in the clouds. When he peered down through it, his face darkened with anger. Dotted across the world below, like little red flowers, were hundreds and hundreds of merrily burning fires.

Zeus roared with rage. "Humans aren't supposed to have fire!" he bellowed. "Only we gods have the power to handle it properly."

He stormed down to earth immediately, and seized the first man he came to by the scruff of the neck. "Who gave you fire?" he demanded.

"Prometheus the titan," the man blurted, turning pale.

"That troublemaker!" Zeus muttered. "I might have guessed." He dropped the man in a heap on the ground and charged away.

Prometheus was at home eating breakfast with Epimetheus, his brother, when Zeus burst through the door. "How dare you give the humans fire!" he thundered.

Epimetheus leaped to his feet in alarm, but Prometheus didn't look the slightest bit worried. "Why shouldn't they have fire?" he asked, rolling his eyes. "I felt sorry for them shivering with cold on dark nights. And I could tell they were tired of eating nothing but raw food."

Zeus turned purple and looked as though he might explode. "It wasn't yours to give," he roared. "You must have stolen it!"

"Yes. That was easy enough," Prometheus boasted. "Yesterday, while you gods were at your party, I lit a stalk from the sun and carried it down to earth." He smirked and added, "I taught the humans how to use fire and how to keep it going. You can't take it back now."

That was more than Zeus was prepared to stand for. "I'll teach you how it feels to have something stolen," he shouted. He grabbed Prometheus by the arm and began to drag him out of the house.

However defiant he was feeling, Prometheus was no match for a god. "Farewell brother," he called to Epimetheus.

"A word of warning: don't take anything from the gods unless you're prepared to face the consequences!"

Zeus took Prometheus to a mountain and chained him there, "You can stay here and take your punishment until you're sorry," he said.

Every day, a giant eagle sent by Zeus would swoop down on the titan. Slowly and agonizingly, it would peck out his liver. But although this would have been painful enough to kill anyone else, Prometheus did not die. Every night, his liver grew back, only for the eagle to arrive the next morning and peck it out all over again.

Amazingly, Prometheus didn't regret what he'd done. "You can torture me until the end of time!" he yelled up at the clouds. "I won't ever be sorry."

Zeus called all the other gods to a meeting in Olympus and told them what had happened. He was furious with the humans for accepting the gift of fire from Prometheus, and had come up with a way to punish them.

Working together, the gods sculpted a perfect woman's figure out of clay. Aphrodite, the goddess of love showered her with beauty. Zeus's daughter, Athena, dressed her in a shimmering gown and Hermes, Zeus's son, hid a bundle of curiosity in her heart. Then, the gods all breathed life into her.

The woman's eyes flickered open and she looked around in wonder. "Who are you?" she asked.

"We are the gods," Zeus answered. "Your name is Pandora. You are to be the wife of a titan named Epimetheus."

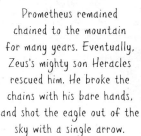

Prometheus remained chained to the mountain for many years. Eventually, Zeus's mighty son Heracles rescued him. He broke the chains with his bare hands, and shot the eagle out of the sky with a single arrow.

He pressed into her hands a large, decorated box. "This is a wedding present," he said. "You may keep it in your house, but you must never open it."

"Why not?" Pandora asked. "What's in it?"

"It's time for you to go now," Hermes told her, ignoring her question and briskly taking her arm. "I'll escort you to your husband's house."

When Epimetheus opened the door of his house to find a beautiful woman and a smiling god standing on the doorstep, his brother's warning vanished entirely from his mind. "Come in, come in," he said to his guests.

He and Pandora got along wonderfully. In fact, they were so in love after an hour of meeting one another, that they arranged to get married that very day.

When the wedding celebrations were over, and the couple went home, Epimetheus noticed the decorated box. "Where did that come from?" he asked his wife.

"It's a wedding gift from Zeus," Pandora replied, picking up the box and staring at it wistfully. "He gave it to me before I'd even met you, and said we must never open it."

"Then we should do as he says," Epimetheus said firmly. He took the box from her and placed it on a shelf.

Pandora nodded but she couldn't help wondering what was inside it. The next time she was alone in the house, she picked it up again and held it in her lap, tracing the decorations on the lid with her fingers. "What use is a box we can't open?" she asked herself. When her husband came home, she put it back hurriedly and said nothing.

One morning a few days later, she was waving goodbye to him through the window, when the box caught her eye again. She sat on the edge of the bed and stared at it for a while. Her curiosity burned inside her.

"Perhaps Zeus meant I shouldn't open it *before* I was married," she said to herself, and she took the box down from the shelf. "What harm can it possibly do if I just have a little look?" She took a deep breath, and opened the lid a tiny crack.

A terrible screeching filled the air and the contents of the box burst out, flinging the lid from her hands. Pandora watched helplessly as hundreds of writhing, horrible things billowed into the air.

They were things that people had never experienced before – war and disease, hatred, malice and jealousy. They whirled around, filling the room, and then seeped out of the open window and spread into the rest of the world.

For a few moments, Pandora was unable to move. She sat staring at the box, numb with despair at what she had done.

Then, as she watched, one last little thing fluttered out. It was pretty and delicate, and not at all like the other things. It flew up out of the window and into the sky, leaving a trail of light behind it. Pandora watched it fly away and, despite herself, she felt her heart lift.

The very last thing that had come out of the box was hope. So, from that moment, although life on earth would never be easy again, no matter what terrible hardships they had to endure, people never gave up hope.

How the seasons came to be

Long ago, when the world was young, there were no such things as seasons. The sun shone and the rain fell in equal measures all year round, and a goddess named Demeter took care of everything that grew. It was she who drew new shoots from the soil and made the flowers bloom, who added the blush to ripe apples and turned the corn golden in the fields.

Demeter had a daughter named Persephone, who was as pretty as a wildflower. Her mother loved her so dearly, she barely ever let her out of sight. But one day something happened that would change that forever.

Persephone was picking violets in a meadow with her friends when the ground beneath them started to shake.

25

Then, with a deafening roar,
the earth split wide open and a chariot
pulled by four jet-black horses burst out
of the chasm. As it thundered past them,
a cloaked figure leaned out and swept
Persephone off her feet.

Persephone's friends could do nothing but watch in horror as the chariot swung around and plunged back into the chasm, taking poor Persephone with it. Then, as suddenly as the opening had appeared, the ground closed up again.

When the girls told Demeter, she rushed to the meadow. The grass was unruffled, betraying no sign that anything had happened. "Tell me who took my daughter," she demanded, pounding the ground in frustration.

The meadow remained silent.

Demeter was inconsolable. For the next year, she searched the world for signs of her daughter, but all in vain. Meanwhile, everything she had tended so lovingly was neglected: the sun shone too harshly and the rain forgot to fall; fruit withered, crops failed and entire forests simply lay down and died. Months passed, and animals and people began to die of starvation. But Demeter didn't even seem to notice.

Eventually the king of the gods, Zeus, summoned her to his palace in the clouds above Mount Olympus. Demeter hurried there, with hope rising in her heart.

"Have you found out who took my daughter?" she asked as soon as she arrived.

"I've known all along who it was," Zeus answered.

"What?" gasped Demeter. "Why didn't you tell me?"

Zeus fixed the goddess with a piercing gaze. "Be honest: you wouldn't give up your daughter for anyone, would you? No matter how suitable a match."

"No man is good enough for her," replied Demeter.

"It's not a man I'm talking about," Zeus said. "It's Hades, god of the Underworld, who took Persephone."

Demeter turned white. "She's in the land of the dead?" she whispered. "It's even worse than I feared."

"How do you know she isn't happy there?" asked Zeus. "Hades is clearly in love with her ... although I admit his courtship may have been a little unusual."

"Unusual?" cried Demeter. "It's unforgivable!"

Zeus sighed. "Then it seems I have little alternative," he muttered. He called to Hermes, the messenger god. "Go down into the Underworld," he told him. "See what you can do to get Persephone back."

Deep in the Underworld, Hermes found Persephone and Hades sitting in a dark, underground garden. Instead of flowers and shrubs, the garden was full of crystals and sparkling gemstones. In fact, there was nothing you'd find in a normal garden, except for one small, twisted fruit tree.

Hades frowned when he saw Hermes. "What brings you here?" he asked.

"Zeus sent me," Hermes answered, sitting down beside Persephone. "How are you?" he asked her gently.

"Hades treats me very well," Persephone replied, glancing at the pale, handsome god at her side. "But living down here in the dark all the time is..." Her voice trailed away as she saw Hades' mournful expression. She looked down at her hands. "I'm terribly homesick. I miss the sunshine and the sky ... and I miss my mother most of all."

Hermes turned to Hades. "You must let her return," he told him.

Hermes, the messenger god, was Zeus's son. As well as acting as a messenger and a go-between, he rather liked helping humans and gods out of tricky situations.

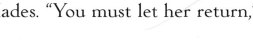

29

The Fates were three goddesses who wove the past, present and future on a large loom.

Clotho spun the thread of life...

...Lachesis measured out a length of thread for each person's life...

...and Atropos cut the thread at the time of a person's death.

"That's impossible," Hades said stubbornly. "I love her. I can't live without her."

"Nor can anyone else," said Hermes sharply. "The Earth is falling to rack and ruin because of her mother's grief. It is Zeus's will that Persephone be returned."

Hades sighed. If it came down to Zeus's will against his own, there was no doubt who would win. Then something occurred to him. "Just a minute," he said. "It's only possible to leave the Underworld if nothing passes your lips while you are here," he said. "The Fates made that rule a long time ago, and it cannot be altered."

"True," Hermes agreed. Even Zeus would not deny the age-old law. "Persephone, have you eaten anything since you've been here?" he asked.

Persephone bit her lip and didn't answer, but her glance strayed to the little fruit tree.

"You shared a pomegranate with me," prompted Hades. "Don't you remember?"

"I only ate six seeds," Persephone protested. "Is that enough to mean I can never go home?"

"But why do you want to leave?" Hades asked. "I've made you my queen. I love you more than anything."

"If you love me so much," Persephone retorted, "you'll let me go home and see my mother."

Hades looked desperately sad. "If I let you go, your mother would never allow you to return," he said quietly. "We'd never, ever see one another again."

Instead of looking glad, as Hermes expected, Persephone suddenly looked very forlorn at the idea.

30

When the couple turned to him for an answer, he said, "The only possible solution is this: for six months of the year, one for every seed she has eaten, Persephone must stay here with you, Hades. For the other six months, she must go home to her mother."

Hades pressed Persephone's hand to his lips with a cry of joy, and she couldn't help but smile.

That year, when Persephone arrived home, the earth blossomed with Demeter's joy. Thousands of green shoots burst through the soil, new leaves unfurled in the trees and flowers sprang into bloom everywhere. All summer long, everything thrived.

But as the time of Persephone's departure drew near, the grass turned brown, flowers faded, and trees shed their leaves like tears. For the six months that Persephone lived in the Underworld, all of nature mourned with Demeter.

Since then, every year has gone through the same cycle: when summer approaches, the earth sings with life; when winter comes, it falls silent again, sorrowfully awaiting the return of spring.

The chariot of the sun

The queen looked down at her son's troubled face and sighed. She knew all too well what he was about to ask her.

"I've been thinking," Phaithon said. "You and I are so alike, you're obviously my mother, but I'm not in the least like the king. Who is my real father?"

His mother could hide the truth from him no longer. "You're right," she said, stroking her son's coppery hair. "You aren't the king's son by birth, although he loves you dearly. Now you are ready to know the truth, I'll tell you. Your real father is Helios, the sun god."

Phaithon glanced at the horizon, where the sun was beginning to set, casting a fiery orange glow into the sky. "Really?" he whispered.

"Really," the queen replied. She gestured to his golden-haired sisters playing on the lawn. "He is your sisters' father too."

Phaithon turned to her, with determination in his eyes.

33

eyes. "I need to meet my real father," he said. "Will you tell me how to find him?"

His mother explained how to reach the sun god's palace, and saddled him a trusty horse to ride. "Come back safely," she called as he set off into the evening, and his sisters all stood in a row and waved goodbye.

Phaithon headed east. He rode all night, until at last, just before morning, he reached the rosy gates of dawn. His father's golden palace rose up majestically behind them. It gleamed so brightly he had to shade his eyes. Leaving his horse at the gates, Phaithon went inside.

He climbed the glittering steps of the palace with his heart in his mouth, and knocked at the vast gold door. When a servant opened it, he said, as boldly as he was able, "Please tell Helios that his son has come to see him."

The servant nodded and disappeared for a few moments. Then he returned, and showed Phaithon through a grand hall, studded with pearls and precious jewels, into another room where a man was sitting on a golden throne. The man was handsome and noble-looking, with bright golden hair and a golden beard. He smiled warmly at the nervous boy, and said, "Phaithon, my son, welcome."

"You know my name!" said Phaithon in surprise.

"I know everything about you," Helios replied. "I have watched you every day since you were born"

Phaithon frowned. "Then why have I never met you?" he asked.

"Come and sit down," Helios said, "and I'll explain. My job, as the sun god, is to drive a chariot carrying the sun across the sky. Early every morning I have to harness up my four horses and set off. I carry the sun up and up to the highest point, and then down the other side of the sky to the west. After sunset, I sail back home on the river of oceans that surround the earth. Then, at dawn, I have to start all over again. If I came to see you, then the sun wouldn't appear in the sky. The whole world would be dark and cold."

"I see," said Phaithon, but his eyes were full of disappointment.

Helios felt a pang of guilt. "Let me make it up to you somehow," he said impulsively. "Name any one thing that would make you feel better, and it's yours."

He smiled as the boy's eyes lit up. But then Phaithon said, "I'd like to take your place for a day. I want to drive your chariot across the sky."

Helios's smile faded, "The horses are fiery-natured and very difficult to control," he said. "Suppose I take you in the chariot with me for the day instead?"

Phaithon shook his head. "I want to do it by myself," he said.

Helios looked at his son in silence for a moment, but he didn't have the heart to turn him down. "Very well," he said at last. "But you must listen very carefully to my instructions. Have you ever driven a chariot before?"

"Hundreds of times," Phaithon lied.

"Good, well that's a start," said his father, and he led him outside to where a team of stablehands was harnessing four lively horses to a golden chariot. Phaithon could barely look at the chariot, for in the back of it sat the enormous, blindingly bright sun.

They walked to the front, and Phaithon beamed at his father, dazzled by the glory of his task. "Don't steer the chariot too high, or you will scorch the heavens," Helios instructed him. "And don't go too low, or you'll burn the earth to a crisp. Phaithon, are you listening to me?"

"Yes, yes," Phaithon said impatiently.

The horses were harnessed but they reared and snorted wildly. Their manes flickered like flames, and fire burned in their eyes. "These horses need a firm hand at all times," Helios said. "If you let them have their heads even for a moment, all will be lost."

The boy climbed into the chariot and took hold of the reins. "You must be careful, Phaithon," Helios told him anxiously.

Phaithon nodded, barely listening in his excitement. The rosy gates of dawn swung open and the horses leaped into action. He let out a yell of exhilaration as the chariot lurched into the open sky.

Driving his father's chariot was better than any dream. As he soared, the sky turned from black to warm blue and the land below was flooded with the sun's golden light. Higher and higher the chariot climbed, and Phaithon felt the power of the horses through the reins as though their strength was his own.

"Faster, faster," he urged them, as they climbed so high that he could almost touch the stars. He flung his head back, thrilled, and gazed at the twinkling constellations

— the great lumbering bear and the bull with its mighty horns.

Phaithon was so busy gazing at the stars that he didn't notice that the horses were climbing far too high. Behind him, the sun was blazing a white-hot trail across the sky. Only when the stars were so close that the bull threatened to gore him with its twinkling horns, did Phaithon look down and gasp.

The earth was suddenly frighteningly far away. Terrified, the boy grappled with the reins, but the strength of the horses was too much for him. They lurched from side to side, and then plunged down, heading straight for the earth. It was all Phaithon could do to hold on.

Down below, people all over the world were watching the sky in horror at the strange and worrying sight of the sun veering from its usual path.

The chariot sped down and down toward the ground. The horses were completely out of control. Phaithon tugged desperately on the reins but he may as well have been an ant for all the effect he had. Just as he thought the chariot was about to crash into the ground, the horses changed direction of their own accord and galloped away wildly, hurtling perilously low over the land.

Now it was so close to the earth the sun's sheer heat set fields of crops and trees ablaze, and scorched vast areas of land into deserts. Rivers began to boil, streams evaporated in puffs of steam, and seas shrank from their shores in the heat.

The white trail the chariot of the sun burned into the sky became known as the Milky Way.

None of this had escaped the notice of the gods. At that very moment, Helios was in Olympus, above the clouds, having been summoned there by Zeus. "What is that boy doing in your chariot?" he demanded, glaring sternly at the lesser god.

"He's my son..." Helios began weakly.

"Oh, never mind the explanation," Zeus interrupted. "The important thing is, how are we going to stop the damage he's doing?"

Helios stared miserably down at the chariot, which was lurching over the mountains, melting deep icy glaciers and causing floods in the valleys beneath them. "It will stop at the end of the day," he said haltingly.

"It's barely midday now!" Zeus snapped. "He could have destroyed the entire planet by this evening. I'm sorry Helios, but there's nothing else to do." He pulled out a thunderbolt, took aim and threw it at the chariot.

Poor Phaithon never knew what hit him. The thunderbolt blasted him from the chariot of the sun. His lifeless body plunged through the sky like a falling star, eventually landing in a wide, winding river.

Without the panic-stricken boy tugging on the reins, the horses gradually calmed down. They galloped on in a fairly straight course across the rest of the sky. However, with nobody to control them, they crossed the sky much more quickly than usual, resulting in an unusually short day.

Helios waited in the west for the empty chariot, tears spilling from his eyes. His horses thundered in, their mouths foaming and their eyes still wide and wild. Through his tears, Helios murmured soothingly, until they came to a shuddering halt in front of him, and lowered their tired heads to nuzzle his outstretched fingers.

Phaithon's poor mother and sisters hurried to the river where he had fallen. Phaithon's mother had realized what must be happening as soon as the sun had started hurtling off course. She had seen the thunderbolt and watched with a sinking heart as a tiny, black speck fell from the sky.

When they reached the river, however, Phaithon's body was long gone. They sank to their knees and wept. His sisters couldn't bring themselves to leave the banks of the river. In fact, they stayed there so long they gradually turned into poplar trees, which continued to weep, and their tears fell as golden amber.

Phaithon's mother returned home alone that night to find Helios waiting on the steps of her palace. She looked at him with empty eyes.

"I can't do anything to bring him back," the sun god said sadly, "and I can't tell you how sorry I am. But I wanted you to know that our son will be remembered. Zeus has placed him among the stars."

He pointed up to the night sky, where a new twinkling constellation of stars had appeared. Ever since then, Phaithon can be seen at night, high in the sky where he had felt so elated.

The constellation came to be known as *Auriga*, which means 'the charioteer'.

Perseus
and the
snake~haired
monster

"I have decided to ask Princess Hippodameia to marry me," King Polydectes announced to his court, completely out of the blue.

One of his younger subjects, Perseus, smiled with relief. For months, the king had been pestering his mother to marry him, but she wasn't the least bit interested. Now he was eighteen, Perseus felt it was his job to protect his mother from unwelcome suitors, even if her admirer was the king himself. Luckily, it seemed the king had turned his attention elsewhere.

"Of course, I'll need to take gifts when I ask for her hand," Polydectes continued. "I wouldn't want her to refuse me." His courtiers laughed politely, and immediately began to offer white horses and fine jewels from their coffers for the king to give his bride-to-be.

Perseus was so busy basking in relief that the king's voice nearly made him jump out of his skin. "And what will you give me, young Perseus?"

In his eagerness for the king's proposal to be accepted, Perseus got rather carried away. "How about a rare orchid from Mount Olympus?" he suggested extravagantly. "Or golden apples from Hera's magic tree? Or I could even bring you the head of Medusa..."

"It's a peculiar engagement gift, but yes, I accept," said the king, cutting him short.

Perseus looked at him questioningly.

"Medusa's head will do nicely," the king said.

Perseus nodded, turning very slightly pale. Medusa was a gorgon — a monstrous creature with a woman's face and hundreds of snakes for hair. Not only that, anyone who met her gaze was instantly turned to stone.

Perseus left the palace feeling as if he had bitten off rather more than he could chew. A sour smile crept over the king's lips as he watched him go. "Now he's out of the way," he muttered darkly, "perhaps his mother will have more time for me."

Perseus was too busy thinking about the task ahead to suspect the king's true intentions. "May the gods help me," he murmured to himself as he walked along. "I haven't the faintest idea where to begin. I don't even know where Medusa lives."

"Only her three sisters can tell you that," said a strange voice above him. Perseus looked up to find a bright-skinned young man hovering in the air. He was wearing sandals with fluttering gold wings which kept him aloft. Perseus stared, open-mouthed – it was Hermes the messenger god.

Hermes smiled. "These will take you to the gorgon's sisters," he said, and handed Perseus a pair of winged sandals just like his own. Then he gave Perseus a bag and a soft, brown cap. "Wearing this cap will make you invisible, so it'll be easier to get close to Medusa," he explained. "It belongs to Hades, so do look after it, won't you? The bag is to carry the head in, should you succeed."

"Th-thank you," stammered Perseus.

"You'll need these as well," came another voice, as Athena, the mighty goddess of war, appeared out of thin air. She handed him a sword and a bronze shield so highly polished that he could see his own astonished face in it. "Good luck," she added. And with that, the god and the goddess vanished.

Perseus eagerly strapped on his new sandals. At once, the tiny wings began to flutter, lifting him off the ground. The next thing he knew, he was soaring high in the sky, far beyond the only kingdom he'd ever known.

He flew for miles across the sea and eventually came within sight of land. The sandals took him down and down, until he landed gently on the pebbled shore at the mouth of a cave.

Perseus heard muffled voices, so he poked his head into the cave and called, "Is anybody home?"

"A visitor, a visitor!" a hoarse voice cried.

Athena wasn't only the goddess of war. She was also the goddess of wisdom, so Perseus was lucky to have her on his side!

"Come in," croaked another.

"Hurry up. Let's see you," said a third.

Inside the cave, Perseus came across the strangest sight he'd had ever seen. Three wrinkled old crones were huddled around a fire. They barely had any teeth, and they only had a single eye between them all. As they spoke they passed it around, each one taking a turn to look at their visitor.

"Why have you come?" asked the one holding the eye.

"Hermes said you could tell me where Medusa lives," replied Perseus.

"Why should we?" demanded another sister, grabbing the eye and thrusting it into Perseus's face to examine him.

"So I can — erm — so I can pay my respects," answered Perseus uncomfortably.

"He's lying," shrieked the crone.

The third snatched the eye and held it up. "You're right," she agreed. "We shouldn't tell him a thing."

"Let me look," said the first crone. But as her sister passed the eye to her, Perseus darted forward and slipped his hand beneath it. The eyeball dropped into his palm.

"Where is it?" demanded the first crone, grasping around in the air.

"I just handed it to you, silly," retorted her sister.

"You must have dropped it," wailed the first.

"Not again," groaned the other sister. "It was weeks before we found it last time."

All three of them began to grope around on the floor for the missing eyeball.

Medusa's sisters were known as the Graeae. They had been white-haired and old since birth.

"It's no use looking down there," said Perseus.

"He's stolen it," screeched one of the crones, and she lunged at him blindly.

Perseus hopped easily out of the way. "Tell me where Medusa lives, and I'll give it back."

"Nooo," howled all three sisters.

"Tell me now," Perseus insisted, "or I'll throw this eyeball into the sea and you'll never find it."

"She's in the forest on the other side of the mountains," blurted one of the sisters, holding out her hand.

Perseus placed the eyeball in her palm. "Thank you," he said, and walked out of the cave, leaving the sisters squabbling over their precious eye.

Filled with confidence after his first success, Perseus leaped into the air. His winged sandals took flight and he soared over the mountains to Medusa's lair.

He reached the forest by sunset. The sun had dyed the sky blood-red and birds were singing farewell to the day. Perseus skimmed low over the treetops, looking for signs of Medusa's cave. He passed over a part of the forest that was strangely cloaked in silence. No birds sang; no leaves rustled with life. Cautiously, he descended through the trees.

He landed on the forest floor and noticed a songbird sitting motionless on a low branch. It had been turned to stone mid-song — its beak was open and he could see every tiny feather on its lifeless breast.

Perseus began to make his way slowly through the trees. Then something stopped him in his tracks. An armed warrior stood in his way — a stone statue with unseeing, stone eyes and an expression of terror on its face. Further along the path was another statue, and then another.

Perseus followed the trail of Medusa's victims until he came to her cave. Quietly, he pulled the cap of invisibility onto his head. Then he drew his sword and stepped into the gloom.

A strange, low hissing noise seeped from the depths of the cave. "That must be her," Perseus thought. "I have to make sure I don't come face-to-face with her, or I'll meet the same end as the others before me..." He held up the polished shield Athena had given him and looked into it. The cave was reflected perfectly, as in a mirror. Looking only at the reflection to guide his way, he headed cautiously in the direction of the noise.

Perseus followed the hissing deeper and deeper into the cave until finally he saw the gorgon herself reflected in the shield. She was lying at the far end of the chamber, fast asleep, all the snakes on her head breathing softly. She was so monstrous that even the sight of her reflection made Perseus's blood run cold.

Sword at the ready, Perseus crept closer and closer. However, just as he drew within striking distance, he stumbled on a rock.

It skittered across the floor and hit the wall with an
echoing crash. Medusa awoke with a jump. "Who goes
there?" she shrieked. She leaped to her feet and the snakes
on her head started writhing around, hissing furiously.
        Perseus stood still and held his breath.
Medusa glared around the cave, but, as Perseus
was invisible, she saw nothing. She took a
    couple of steps forward and Perseus
        seized his chance.

He swung his sword as hard as he could at her neck. But it was difficult to judge the distance, looking only at a reflection. His sword lopped off several snakes, but it missed her neck by a good few inches.

Medusa glared wildly in Perseus's direction and he felt the stony power of her gaze boring through him. "I know you're there. Reveal yourself, coward," she taunted. "Are you too afraid to look me in the eyes?"

Perseus kept his eyes firmly on his shield. Quietly, he picked up a rock and tossed it across the cave. It landed with a crash, and Medusa spun around towards the sound and pounced. Perseus sprang at her and, as quick as a flash, sliced through her neck. Her head rolled onto the floor, eyes wide open, and the snakes fell limp and silent.

Careful not to meet Medusa's gaze, even in death, Perseus picked up the head by its snake hair and put it carefully into the bag. He was about to set off, when he heard a noise outside the cave. He froze as two other gorgons came inside. "Medusa," one of them called. "Are you awake?"

Perseus, still invisible, pressed himself against the wall of the cave as they passed. "Who did this?" screamed one, as she saw Medusa's headless body sprawled on the floor. The other let out such a piercing moan that rocks began to crack and crumble from the roof of the cave.

Perseus edged out of the cave unseen, and took flight. As he rose high into the sky, the realization of his success filled him with dizzying delight. He swept over the forest, soared over the tops of the mountains, glided over

After Perseus killed Medusa and left her cave, something very strange happened. Out of the neck of Medusa's body a pure white, winged horse, named Pegasus, was born. It flew out of the cave and lived wild in the forest until a young man named Bellerophon tamed it many years later.

48

the sea, crossed the flame-hot desert, and skimmed low over the coast beyond, cooling his face in the sea breeze.

When he reached Greece, he went straight to his mother. "I'm so glad you're safe," she said, hugging him tightly. But then she said, "I have bad news though, I'm afraid. I have to marry the king today. I can refuse only on pain of death."

"But he's supposed to be marrying Princess H..." Perseus began, and then he realized his mistake. "I'll see about that," he said, and marched off to the palace right away, with the bag containing Medusa's head still slung over his shoulder.

When he presented himself before the king, a murmur of surprise rippled around the assembled crowd. King Polydectes eyed him coldly. "What are you doing here?" he demanded.

"I've brought you Medusa's head," Perseus replied, "as I said I would."

"Nonsense," the king snorted. "You could never kill Medusa! Do you even know how many real men have tried and failed?"

"I have the head right here if you'd like to see it," said Perseus, his voice simmering with anger.

"Show me," ordered the king.

"Everyone who believes me," warned Perseus, "look away now." And he held up Medusa's head. Many people averted their eyes. But the king and all his courtiers were turned to stone where they sat, with ugly expressions of horror and disbelief fixed on their faces forever.

As Perseus flew over the Libyan Desert, a few drops of blood fell from Medusa's head. They landed on some snakes, filling them with terrible poison. There have been deadly snakes living there ever since.

49

Echo
and
Narcissus

Echo was a mountain nymph, and a terrible chatterbox. All day and almost all night, streams of words would pour from her lips. It wasn't as if she always had something sensible to say. Most of the time it was nonsense. She didn't mean any harm, but her constant babble could be rather irritating.

One summer's afternoon, Echo was chattering away to herself as she wandered through the mountains where she lived. "Isn't it a lovely day? Oh, just look at the sunlight on the trees, doesn't it make you smile," she burbled.

All of a sudden, the goddess Hera appeared, bustling down the mountain path in a tremendous hurry. She stopped when she saw Echo. "Have you seen my husband?" she demanded.

"Oh hello Hera, isn't it a lovely day? I was just saying how lovely it was when…" Echo began.

51

"Never mind all that," Hera interrupted crossly. "Have you seen my husband?"

"Zeus? Why of course, I've met him once or twice," Echo babbled. "He's a very handsome god, I always thought. I don't know of any two gods who suit one another more..."

"Have you seen him *today?*" shouted Hera, turning red in the face with frustration.

"It would be just as pleasant to see him today as any other," Echo replied brightly. "I think it would be pleasant to see just about anyone today..."

Hera couldn't stand it any longer. She seized the nymph by the scruff of the neck. "Stop talking such nonsense!" she yelled. "From now on you won't be able to prattle on like this to anyone. In fact you won't be able to say anything at all, apart from repeating what anyone else says to you. Is that absolutely clear?"

"Absolutely clear," said Echo, as timidly as a mouse.

Hera let go of her and stormed away.

Echo spent the rest of the day alone and in silence, unable to speak a word. At first she thought she might be suffering from shock. But the next morning, she tried to speak and she still couldn't squeeze a single sound past her lips. Her heart sank. Hera had meant every word.

Only when a little bird landed on a nearby branch and twittered merrily at her could poor Echo speak. "Tweet, tweet," she repeated miserably back to the bird.

Later that day, she was wandering silently along a rocky path, when she bumped into a young man coming around the corner. He was so handsome she stopped in her tracks and smiled at him. It was love at first sight.

Unfortunately for Echo, the young man was so handsome that he was used to people falling in love with him, and it had done his character no good whatsoever.

"What do you want?" he asked rather rudely.

"You want you want you..." was all Echo could say.

"Want me, do you? Everybody wants me, I'm Narcissus!" scoffed the vain young man. "What makes you think I could love you?"

"I could love you," Echo repeated hopefully.

"Well I could never love you," snapped Narcissus.

"Love you," was Echo's sad reply.

Poor Echo was so in love with Narcissus, that she couldn't bear to leave him. She trailed after him, unable to say anything other than repeat whatever he said. Narcissus grew very tired of her and because he wasn't the kindest of young men, he told her so, in no uncertain terms.

Eventually, unable to get rid of her, Narcissus simply took to ignoring her. He was thirsty from all the walking he'd done that day, so when he came to a clear mountain pool, he crouched down to drink from the still water.

As he drank, the sun came out from behind a cloud and shone brightly into the pool, showing Narcissus his own reflection. He'd never seen it before. And now as he bent to drink, it looked as if his lips were meeting those of another person leaning toward him in the pool. He sat back in surprise. "Did you just kiss me?" he asked the face, blushing with pleasure.

Looking every bit as surprised as he was,
the face in the pool mouthed the same words.

"I don't mind," Narcissus said shyly. "I think
you're beautiful."

"You're beautiful," Echo repeated wistfully behind
him. But Narcissus only had eyes for the face in the pool.
He smiled, and as the face smiled back at him, the young
man felt a fire rising in his chest that he had never felt
before. He had fallen head over heels in love with his
own reflection.

He bent forward in a rush to kiss the face again,
but in his eagerness, he broke the calm surface of the pool
and the face disappeared. Narcissus was filled with despair.
"Won't you be mine?" he cried out.

"Be mine," Echo repeated mournfully.

The water fell still and the reflection appeared once
more. Narcissus stared at the sad face before him. Tears
welled up in the boy's eyes just like those in his own. It was
then that Narcissus realized who the face was. "It's me,"
he whispered. "I'm in love with Narcissus."

"I'm in love with Narcissus," repeated Echo's barely audible voice.

Despite realizing his mistake, Narcissus still couldn't drag himself away from his own reflection. He remained there, staring longingly into the pool until night fell. When the moon came out, he rejoiced in the reflection's dim reappearance, and when the sun finally rose, he smiled in relief at himself. Day after day he lay there beside the pool, the rest of the world entirely forgotten.

Echo couldn't bear to leave either. She watched with despair as the young man she loved grew pale and thin. Gradually, the bloom faded from Echo's own cheeks, and her face paled until she could barely be seen in the harsh sunlight. In fact, soon her body itself began to fade. Gradually, she pined away for her love, until she was nothing but a voice on the breeze, repeating its every sigh.

Not that Narcissus noticed. He was completely absorbed in himself. He watched his own cheeks grow paler and thinner, and his eyes burn ever more feverishly with love.

Eventually, Narcissus dwindled away to nothing at all. In his place, by the side of the pool, a yellow flower grew, which has been known by his name ever since.

As for Echo, her voice remained, blown by the wind to different parts of the world. Being a mountain nymph, she prefers to haunt mountainous or rocky places.

If you call out in places such as those, sometimes you may hear her mournfully repeating your words back to you.

The narcissus flower (or daffodil) can often be found growing beside pools of water, admiring its own reflection.

How spiders came to be

Arachne's fingers moved so quickly across the loom they were a blur. She hummed as she wove, passing the shuttle expertly back and forth, and onlookers jostled for space as they watched the tapestry take shape. In no time at all it was finished.

"What do you think of that?" she said, handing the piece to a shy nymph who had ventured out from the forest to see the famous girl at work. The tapestry showed animals playing among the trees, and had a border of intertwined leaves all around.

"It's lovely," breathed the nymph. "You must be better at weaving than anyone else in the world."

Arachne nodded proudly, "I'm better than any of the gods too, actually," she boasted.

A frail voice spoke up from the crowd. "You can't be better than the goddess Athena – she's famous for her weaving. You're only human, after all."

"I can weave better than she can," snorted Arachne.

The old lady who had spoken stepped forward.

57

"That's rather a bold claim," she said, her voice sharpening. "I'd take it back if I were you. You never know who's listening."

"I wouldn't care if Athena herself could hear me," Arachne said scornfully. "I stand by what I say."

The old woman threw back the hood of her cape and straightened her back. The wrinkles on her face faded until her skin was smooth and glowing; she grew taller and her hair became glossy. Before the crowd's very eyes, she turned into the goddess Athena.

Everyone bowed their heads respectfully, apart from Arachne, who just stared at the goddess, first flushing red and then turning very pale.

"Do you dare repeat that to my face?" Athena asked.

An angry goddess is a terrifying sight, but Arachne was far too proud to back down. Her voice wavered a little as she spoke. "I can weave better than you can," she said.

Athena's eyes narrowed. "Then let's have a competition and you can prove it to everyone."

Arachne nodded, swallowing nervously. She stood up from her loom and gestured to the stool. "You can go first, if you like," she said.

Athena sat down, pushed back her sleeves, and began to weave. As everyone watched, the threads started to form a beautiful, intricate scene. It showed arrogant humans being put in their place by the glorious gods. The figures were so lifelike that when she wove Zeus throwing a thunderbolt in anger, people in the crowd ducked, thinking the bolt was about to hit them.

Beneath her fingers, the thread somehow glowed brighter than any ordinary thread. And when she had finished, the image shimmered as though it was inlaid with gold and silver. It was truly amazing.

"There," Athena said triumphantly. And she stood up to let Arachne take her place at the loom.

Arachne took a deep breath and began to weave. She worked intently, without saying a word, and as she wove, people gasped at her skill. She had never produced anything more wonderful – or more daring – than this.

The scene she wove was every bit as intricate as Athena's, but it showed brave heroes challenging foolish gods. Tiny ships sailed valiantly across the seas, while Zeus stirred up a storm looking for all the world like a giant, truculent toddler.

When Arachne had finished, she turned to the crowd. "Well?" she said. There was no denying her skill. The tapestry was every bit as good as Athena's, if not better. But nobody was fool enough to say so.

Athena's face was as menacing as a thundercloud. "Your arrogance will be your downfall," she shouted. She tore the tapestry from the loom and ripped it into tiny shreds in front of Arachne's face. Then she seized the girl by the throat and lifted her up into the air. "How dare you challenge a goddess and expect to win?" she hissed. "I'll see to it that you never weave again."

Arachne's face turned ashen as she gasped for breath. "Please," she begged hoarsely. "Weaving is all I've ever wanted to do. It's all I *can* do."

Athena dropped the girl in a crumpled heap on the floor. "Fine," she snapped. "You may continue weaving. But you certainly won't be able to boast about it any more." She rapped the girl on the top of her head with her knuckles, and at once, a terrible transformation began to take place.

Arachne's arms and legs shrank back into her body, leaving only her eight long fingers along her sides. Her head squashed into her torso which became squat and round. Her nose disappeared entirely and her eyes multiplied until she had eight of them in a row. Her skin turned dark and sprouted hairs, and she shrank and shrank until she was no bigger than the palm of a child's hand. Arachne had turned into a spider.

She scuttled away into the shadows, and everyone thought they had seen the last of her. But the very next morning, a nymph came running from the forest. "Come and see," she shouted excitedly.

The villagers followed her back to the forest where the nymph showed them a beautiful woven pattern hanging between the branches. The thread was so delicate a mere breath could break it, and the pattern was dotted with dew drops that glittered in the sun like diamonds. The skill was unmistakable.

"Arachne the spider has woven her first web," the nymph announced.

From that day forward, evidence of Arachne's weaving has been found all over the world. So many webs have been found in so many far-flung places, that people say Arachne must have passed on her skill to lots of other spiders, too.

Heracles, the strongest man in the world

Y ou could tell Heracles was the son of Zeus
just by looking at him. He was so strong that,
by the time he was five, he could lift a carthorse
above his head, much to the delight of his friends.

Zeus's wife, the goddess Hera, hated him. He was
Zeus's son with a human woman, rather than with her, and
the very sight of him made her blood boil with jealousy.

When he was a baby, she had sent two poisonous
snakes to his cradle to kill him. But Heracles had just
giggled and strangled the life out of them with his tiny fists.
She had felt like blasting him to smithereens there and
then, but she knew Zeus would only hate her for it.

So Hera swallowed her spite and waited for another
opportunity to get rid of him.

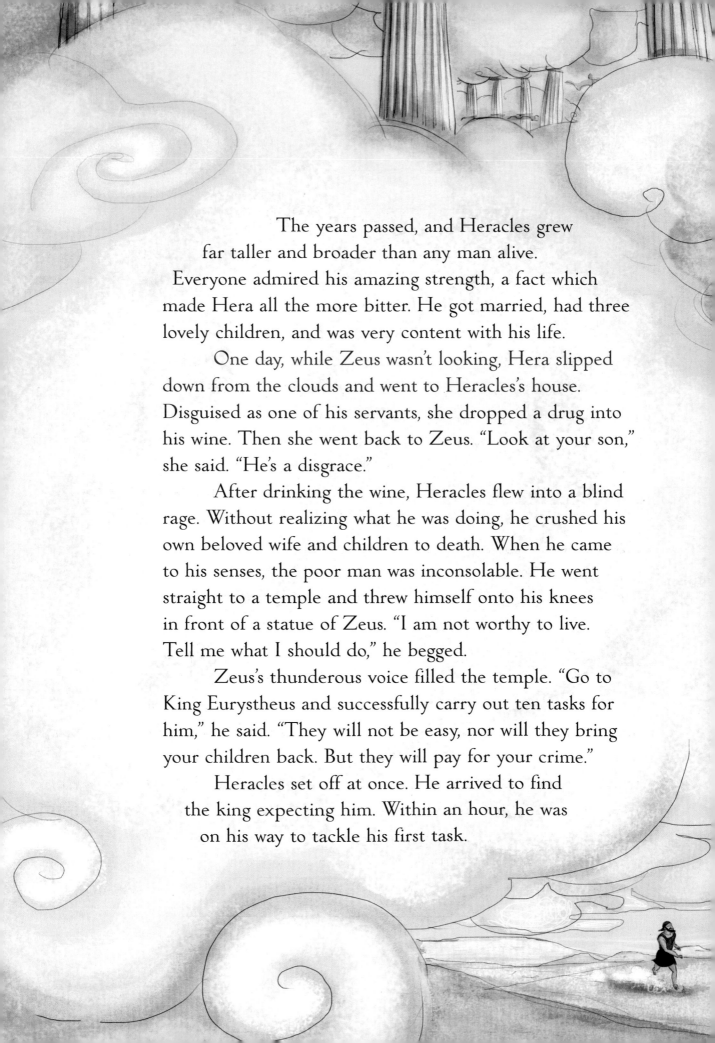

The years passed, and Heracles grew
far taller and broader than any man alive.
Everyone admired his amazing strength, a fact which
made Hera all the more bitter. He got married, had three
lovely children, and was very content with his life.

One day, while Zeus wasn't looking, Hera slipped
down from the clouds and went to Heracles's house.
Disguised as one of his servants, she dropped a drug into
his wine. Then she went back to Zeus. "Look at your son,"
she said. "He's a disgrace."

After drinking the wine, Heracles flew into a blind
rage. Without realizing what he was doing, he crushed his
own beloved wife and children to death. When he came
to his senses, the poor man was inconsolable. He went
straight to a temple and threw himself onto his knees
in front of a statue of Zeus. "I am not worthy to live.
Tell me what I should do," he begged.

Zeus's thunderous voice filled the temple. "Go to
King Eurystheus and successfully carry out ten tasks for
him," he said. "They will not be easy, nor will they bring
your children back. But they will pay for your crime."

Heracles set off at once. He arrived to find
the king expecting him. Within an hour, he was
on his way to tackle his first task.

I
The Nemean lion

When a huge, hulking stranger walked through the town of Nemea, the locals stared at him goggle-eyed. He was a giant of a man, who couldn't fail to attract attention but, in addition to that, he was heading out of town on a road nobody else dared use.

"Don't go that way," a trader called after him. "There's a lion down there that'll tear you to pieces, big as you are."

"I've been sent to kill that lion," the stranger said.

The trader gulped. "It can't be killed," he said. "Swords and arrows just bounce off its skin."

The stranger shrugged. "I won't use swords or arrows," he said, and continued on his way.

"What's your name?" called the trader. "So we know who to hold a funeral for later."

"Heracles," the stranger answered over his shoulder.

A little further down the road, Heracles stopped by the opening of a cave that was littered with splintered white bones. In a blur of tawny fur, the lion shot out of the cave and pounced. Powerful muscles rippled under its skin as it bore down on Heracles, opening its jaws to reveal an impressive set of teeth.

Heracles plucked the creature out of the air, wrestled it to the ground and snapped its neck with his bare hands. Without further ado, he slung the dead lion over his shoulder, and trudged back the way he'd come.

"That was quick!" the king exclaimed when Heracles flung the lion's body at his feet. Even stone dead it still looked fairly frightening.

Heracles shrugged. "What do you want me to do with it?" he asked flatly.

"Whatever you like," the king replied. So Heracles used the beast's own claws to skin it, and made a cloak for himself to wear. He slung the cloak around his shoulders. "What's next?" he asked.

After slaying the Nemean lion, Heracles wore its skin as a cloak on all his adventures. Not only did it make the warrior hero look even more impressive, but it also protected him against swords and arrows.

II
The many~headed hydra

"Your next task is to slay a monster called the hydra," announced King Eurystheus. "It lives in a swamp and has more heads than anyone has ever been able to count."

Heracles tucked his sword into his belt and set off. He hadn't gone far when a chariot drew up beside him. It was his nephew, Iolaus. "Uncle, let me drive you," offered the boy.

"No," said Heracles gruffly. "I don't want to put you in any danger," he said. "These tasks are my responsibility."

"I know," Iolaus answered. "But I want to help."

Heracles looked at him in silence for a moment. Then he grasped Iolaus's outstretched hand and climbed into the chariot.

When they came to the edge of the swamp, they found the hydra's tracks in the wet ground. They followed them to the mouth of a deep, dark tunnel. Heracles collected some damp branches, set fire to them and threw them into the opening. The tunnel filled with smoke, and before long the monster slithered out.

It was enormous, with a long, serpentine body and countless heads that writhed around, poison dripping from their fangs. Iolaus dived for cover behind the chariot as the hydra reared up over them.

Heracles sliced off the nearest of its heads with his sword, and dodged the others as they lunged at him. He was so busy avoiding them that he didn't see the severed neck spring two new heads behind him.

"Look out!" Iolaus yelled, and Heracles turned and flung up his shield as the two new heads attacked. He chopped them off, but four heads sprouted in their place.

Frowning, Heracles began a determined assault. He whirled his sword as fast as he could, trying to chop off all the heads before any more sprouted. But each time he lopped one head off, two sprang up in its place.

It was an impossible task. Every time he succeeded in severing a head, he only made the situation worse. In no time at all, Heracles could barely see past the snaking forest of poison-tipped fangs. It was all he could do to shield himself from being bitten.

Then he had an idea. "Throw me a fire brand," he shouted to his nephew. Quick as a flash, Iolaus lit a dry branch and tossed it to him. Heracles caught it, sliced another of the creature's heads off and quickly pressed the branch to its neck. The monster let out a horrific scream as the fire touched its skin. The flames sealed the wound, and no more heads sprouted from the neck.

Heracles launched himself into lopping off the monster's heads and branding its necks. It was nearly night by the time the last head rolled into the swamp and the hydra's body slumped in a heap in the mud.

After tossing it into the back of the chariot, Heracles climbed in beside his waiting nephew. Iolaus's chest swelled with pride, as he drove Heracles back to the palace.

"Very good," said the king, when he was presented with the huge, headless body. Then he pointed at Iolaus. "Who is this?" he asked. "Did he help you?"

Heracles smiled. "Yes, this is my nephew. He passed me a fire brand which I used to seal the monster's necks."

"Then I'm afraid this task doesn't count," said the king. "You have to complete them all without any help."

Heracles shot the king an angry look, but he pressed his lips together and said nothing. He took a deep breath before he spoke again. "Fine," he said. "What's next?"

III
The golden~horned stag

Heracles had been chasing the Ceryneian stag for a year and a day before he eventually caught up with it. With all his muscles weighing him down, he wasn't really suited for running.

Finally, he was so close that he could hear it panting

with exhaustion as it struggled to swim across a river.
He strode into the water and waded after it. But before he
was even halfway across, the stag was already scrambling
up the opposite bank.

"There was no way I'm letting you get away now,"
he muttered under his breath. He planted his legs firmly
against the rushing water, fitted an arrow to his bow and
took aim. He didn't dare harm the creature. It belonged
to the goddess Artemis, and besides, his task was to bring
it to the king alive. So he aimed low and fired.

The arrow clipped one of the stag's ankles, which
was just enough to slow it down. Heracles waded across
the water, climbed the bank and lifted it gently onto
his shoulders.

Just as he was beginning the long walk back to the
king's palace, a noble-looking woman rode up to him on a
moon-white horse. She had a strange glow about her skin
that made him realize she was no ordinary woman. "What
are you doing with my stag?" she said. Her voice was as
sharp as any arrow.

Heracles knelt before her and bowed his head.
"Noble goddess, Artemis," he said humbly. "I know that
you could have struck me down by now for even touching
this creature of yours. So perhaps you will be merciful
when I explain that I have no choice. I am bound by the
tasks set me by King Eurystheus. However, I promise I will
set your stag free once I have shown it to the king."

The goddess stared at him coldly for a moment.
"If you do not," she said, "then I will find you and flay the

skin from your limbs." She turned her horse and rode away, her hair streaming out behind her.

Heracles watched her go. Then he got to his feet and made his way back to the palace. He showed the stag to the king, then took it outside and set it free.

IV
The giant wild boar

"You can catch a harmless stag and bring it to me alive," said the king, "but how about something a little more dangerous? There's a giant wild boar that lives on Mount Erymanthos. Bring it to me without harming a single bristle on its body."

"That should keep him busy for a while," he thought to himself as he watched Heracles leave.

An angry voice behind him made him jump. "That won't take any time at all. It's far too easy."

The king swung around to find himself face to face with the goddess Hera. He didn't know what to say. He had received his orders from Zeus to set Heracles the tasks. He hadn't realized the god's wife was involved too. "It's... it's a very large, fierce boar..." he began.

"It'll be child's play to him," she snapped. "You're not supposed to be setting him tasks he'll enjoy. See to it that the next one is tougher." And with that, she vanished.

Only an hour later, there was a terrible squealing and bellowing, as Heracles entered the palace with a terrifyingly huge, red-eyed boar across his shoulders. The king climbed into a big pot in fright.

"Don't worry," laughed Heracles as the king peered nervously out of the neck of the pot. "It's tied up."

V

The stinking stables

"Cleaning out stables is hardly equal to the other tasks I've been set," Heracles muttered indignantly as he approached King Augeas's palace grounds. Nonetheless, he had agreed to carry out all King Eurystheus's orders, so he couldn't refuse.

He wrinkled his nose at the terrible stench in the air. The closer he got to the palace, the more unbearable the smell became. He came to a herd of cattle huddled miserably near a river at the top of a sloping field. At the bottom of the hill there was another river and a large stable building. Great heaps of dung spilled out of doors at either end of the stables, which were barely visible through the cloud of dark flies that surrounded them.

"There's no way the owner of this mess deserves to have it cleaned up for nothing," Heracles thought. He went into the palace and asked to see the king. A servant showed him to a pristine throne room, where King Augeas was sitting with his young nephew.

"I was just passing," Heracles announced, "and I couldn't help noticing the state of your stables. I can clean them out for you for some payment, if you like. Say a quarter of your herd?"

"They are rather dirty," admitted King Augeas. "Alright, it's a deal."

The king and his nephew followed the stranger outside to watch. Heracles wrapped a scarf around his nose and mouth and then marched to the stables. Using a long branch broken from a nearby tree, he prodded open the doors at both ends of the stables, without having to wade through the muck. Then he trudged away and brought back a shovel.

First, Heracles dug a trench from the doors at the lower end of the stables down to the river below. Then, he dug a second trench from the doors at the other end of the stables, up to meet the river at the top of the hill.

As he broke the river's banks with his shovel, the water gushed into the trench. It flowed, foaming and curling, down the channel Heracles had dug, right through the stables, washing away all the dung into the river below.

Heracles stood back and watched with a smile of satisfaction. When every last trace of filth had gone, he filled in the upper trench again, and allowed the river to resume its normal course.

Augeas's nephew gasped in awe. "You didn't even get your hands dirty!" exclaimed the king.

"There was no need," said Heracles. "So should I take my share of the cattle with me now?"

"Er – no," said the king. "You're not taking any of my cattle."

"But you agreed to give him a quarter of the herd," his nephew protested.

"I've got an army ready that will agree I didn't," warned the king.

Heracles shook his head. "That's a disgraceful way to behave," he said. "But I didn't come here for a fight."

He walked away, but the king's nephew ran after him. "Could I give you a lift home?" he said. "It's the least I can offer." Heracles agreed, so they went together back to King Eurystheus's palace.

"Did you clean King Augeas's stables?" the king asked Heracles when they arrived.

"I did," Heracles replied.

"I can vouch for that," added the nephew. "I saw it with my own eyes. But my awful uncle refused to pay up. Perhaps you could persuade him?"

King Eurystheus narrowed his eyes. "You aren't to ask for payment, Heracles," he said sternly. "That's it. You've forfeited this task. It doesn't count."

Heracles clenched his fists in frustration, but bowed his head and said nothing.

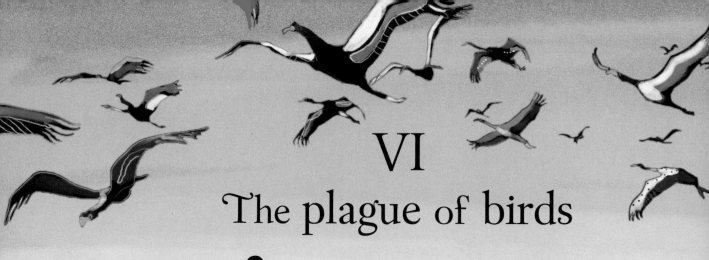

VI
The plague of birds

"Next you must catch and kill all the birds at Lake Stymphalis," said the king. "These birds are a plague on all the fruit farmers nearby."

Heracles nodded. "Very well," he said.

The villages and farms that surrounded the lake were in a pitiful state. Every last tree and field for miles around was stripped entirely bare of leaves as well as fruit. Although it was the middle of summer, there weren't any crops to be seen.

Heracles sat by the lake for a while, staring thoughtfully at the flocks of birds roosting in trees all around it. When he had come up with a plan, he strode into the nearest village.

He stopped at each house and asked to borrow as many metal items and ropes as the villagers could spare. Then he sat in the marketplace and started tying them all together. As he worked, a ragged group of children gathered around him to watch.

"Is your name Heracles?" a skinny boy asked.

Heracles nodded.

"Then you're the man who killed the hydra," the boy said enthusiastically. "You're great."

"Not so very great," Heracles said gently.

Using all the metal he had collected, he made

the biggest rattle the children had ever seen. He lifted it carefully above his head and walked back to the edge of the lake. All the children followed him to watch.

First, Heracles got his bow and arrows ready, and then he shook the rattle as hard as he could. The sudden clanking and clattering it made was so shockingly loud that all the birds flew up into the sky in alarm.

Immediately, Heracles began to shoot them down in a shower of arrows. He shot with such force that each arrow speared four or five birds. He shot so quickly and accurately, that not a single bird escaped. In no time at all, every one had fallen.

Heracles went back to the village with the children holding his hands and skipping along in front of him. He returned all the metal things to the villagers, and was richly rewarded in smiles and hugs of thanks.

VII
The bull from Crete

Heracles returned to the palace happier than he had felt in years. He smiled at the king and said, "What would you like me to do next?"

"Bring me the famous bull from Crete," the king replied. "Apparently it's so handsome the queen there fell in love with it. I want to see it for myself."

"No problem," said Heracles. He sailed to Crete, where he found the enormous, heavily muscled bull in a meadow near the palace. He knocked on the door of the palace and asked King Minos whether he could borrow it. "You can have it," said the king. "It's of no use to me."

So Heracles picked up the bull in one hand, as though it were as light as a kitten. He carried it to his ship and sailed back.

"It's a handsome bull," said King Eurystheus when Heracles carried it in to show him, "but I can't understand why a queen would fall in love with it." Heracles shrugged. "The world is a very strange place," he said.

Watching from the clouds, the goddess Hera rolled her eyes in annoyance. "That king's hopeless," she muttered. "If I want Heracles to fail these tasks, I'm going to have to see to it myself."

VIII
The man-eating mares

Nobody knew where they had come from, but word spread fast – the King of Thrace had a stable full of man-eating mares. The king's enemies, any unwelcome visitors and pretty much anyone who displeased him ended up being fed to these horses. Everyone was terrified of getting on the wrong side of the king. He was becoming a complete tyrant.

Heracles set sail for Thrace, under orders to put an end to it once and for all. When he arrived, he went straight to the king and introduced himself. "I have heard of your great hospitality," he said innocently, "and wondered whether you might let me stay the night."

"Certainly," said the king with a sly smile. "Perhaps you would like to come riding with me before dinner, and I can show you some of my beautiful country."

"I'd be delighted," Heracles replied, and he followed the king to the stables.

"I was given some very unusual horses as a gift by the goddess Hera," said the king. He opened the door a crack to let Heracles inside. "After you," he smiled.

"No, no," Heracles said, pushing the king into the stable and bolting the door behind him. "After you."

There was a scream and the sound of neighing and stomping hooves. When the noise died away, Heracles looked inside the stable to find seven large mares standing with their heads hung low. They had blood around their mouths and looked rather sick and dejected. There was no trace of the king.

"He can't have tasted very good," Heracles said to them. "Perhaps that'll teach you not to eat flesh." He led the mares outside to the meadow, where they began to nibble on the fresh green grass. After that, they were as harmless as ordinary horses for the rest of their days.

IX
Queen of the Amazons

"Your next task is to sail to the land of the Amazons and bring back their queen's belt," said King Eurystheus. Heracles looked up in interest. The Amazons were a people known for their strength and prowess in war. They lived far away and so Heracles had never met any, but it was said that all their warriors were women. "What's so good about her belt?" he asked.

"It's supposed to make the wearer invincible," explained the king.

"Very well," said Heracles. "I'll get it for you."

He set sail that afternoon, and was at sea for many days, until he reached the land of the Amazons. As soon as he drew into the port, he noticed that there wasn't a single man to be seen. All the women were tall and muscular. They carried bows over their shoulders and javelins strapped to their backs, as if they might spring into battle at any moment.

Heracles was eyed with suspicion as he moored his ship. He went up to the nearest woman and announced, "I have come in peace to meet your queen."

The woman gave him an unwelcoming frown. "You'll find her palace at the top of that street," she said, pointing up into the city.

Heracles thanked her and went to present himself

to the queen. He was shown into the palace, where he found a noble-looking woman sitting on a throne with a crowd of other women around her. The queen was even more powerfully built than the others, with tanned skin and glinting green eyes. Like the other women, she was armed with a bow and a javelin, but in addition to this she wore a large, decorated leather belt around her waist. Heracles had never seen anyone like her. But she seemed to recognize him right away.

The Amazon queen's magical belt was said to have been a gift from her father, Ares, the god of war and strength.

"Mighty Heracles," she said. Seeing his look of surprise, she explained: "Tales of your many adventures precede you. In fact, they make you sound almost strong enough to join our number." A ripple of laughter passed around the room. "Of course being a man, you could never be quite up to our standard," the queen added with a twinkle in her eye.

Heracles smiled. "Tales of your many adventures are told in my land, too," he said politely. "I would much rather be your friend than your enemy."

"Tell me, what brings you here?" the queen asked.

"I am under a king's command to bring home your belt," Heracles answered. "My king seems to think it's the source of all your success," he added. "But, now I've met you, I think you are probably strong enough without it."

The queen laughed. "So you think you can flatter me out of it, do you?" she said. "Clever Heracles. Somehow I can't resist. You're absolutely right – I don't need this belt to make me strong." She unbuckled her belt and laid it on a table. "I'll tell you what. If you beat me in an arm-wrestle,"

81

she said, "you may take it home with my blessing."

Heracles had never had any trouble beating anyone in a simple arm-wrestle, and he presumed a woman – even a strong one – would be an easy opponent. So he sat down opposite the queen. They placed their elbows on the table and joined hands.

"Go," said the queen. Heracles pushed a little, expecting her arm to collapse right away. She stared coolly into his eyes, and her arm didn't move an inch. Heracles strained a little harder, and the muscles bulged in both of their arms, but the queen's arm still didn't move. It was only after twenty minutes of concentrated effort, with the veins bulging in his forehead and his arm muscles quivering with the strain, that he finally managed to push her arm down onto the table. "You're a worthy opponent indeed," he said.

"You aren't bad yourself," the Queen admitted good-naturedly, pushing the belt across the table. They shook hands and Heracles left the palace taking the belt with him. He was making his way through the town back to the port, when a cry came from nearby. "That stranger has stolen the queen's belt. Stop! Thief!"

Everyone within earshot rushed at Heracles, their weapons drawn. Before Heracles realized what was happening, someone had snatched the belt from his hands and he was surrounded by a field of javelin tips.

Heracles whipped out his sword and fought the Amazons back, driving off ten or twelve at a time. They shot arrows and threw javelins at him, but Heracles whirled

his sword around, slicing them to pieces as they reached him. "Your queen gave me that belt," he roared angrily. "Would you go against her will?"

The Amazons hesitated in their attack, unsure whether his claim was true. Then a noble-looking woman at the front of the group said, "Why ever would my sister give her belt to a stranger?" She jabbed her javelin at Heracles so fiercely that it stuck fast in his shield.

He pulled on the shield sharply, making her stumble towards him. Then he slipped behind her and held his sword at her throat.

"Tell the queen that I have captured her sister," he told the others. "I will let her have what is hers, if I may have back what is rightfully mine." One of the Amazons ran off with the message. Five minutes later, she returned. "The queen sends her apologies," she reported. "The belt is yours. She asks you to release her sister unharmed."

The belt was handed back to Heracles, and he let go of the queen's sister. "Thank you," he said.

The crowd of Amazons parted to let him walk the rest of the way to his ship, and watched as he set sail. "Nobody has ever beaten me before," said the queen's sister, frowning after the ship. "Who was that extraordinary man?"

"That was Heracles, son of Zeus," a voice answered. It belonged to the woman who had called Heracles a thief and started the attack. She didn't look at all like an Amazon. She was just as tall and powerful, but instead of tanned skin, hers was whiter than marble and glowed with an unearthly radiance. It was the goddess Hera. "I must admit he's beginning to win my respect," she muttered.

Before the Amazons could ask the beautiful stranger who she was, she melted away into the crowd and was not seen again.

Heracles sailed home and presented the belt to King Eurystheus. Stories of his single-handed conquest of the Amazon queen spread like wildfire throughout the land.

X
Geryon's red cattle

"Your next task is to bring me Geryon's red cattle," King Eurystheus ordered Heracles.

"How will I find them?" Heracles asked.

"You can't miss them," answered the king. "Not only are they scarlet, but Geryon is a three-bodied giant. His dog, which guards the herd, has two heads. You'll find them on the red isle of Erytheia."

It took Heracles months to get to the red isle. On the way, he slew a good few monsters just for the exercise. He grew stronger than ever before and, wherever he went, people seemed to have heard all about him and the tasks he was performing.

Eventually he reached Libya, where the sun was so hot he felt as if it would bake his brain inside his head.

"This heat will drive me crazy," he said, frowning up at the burning sun. He took aim with his arrow, ready to shoot it out of the sky.

Before he could, there was a blinding flash of light, and a glowing golden figure appeared beside him. "You've certainly got pluck, trying to shoot me down," the figure chuckled and Heracles realized with a jolt that it was the sun god, Helios.

Luckily, Helios was amused, rather than offended, and when he heard that Heracles was trying to reach the distant red isle, he lent him a giant golden cup to sail in.

"It's the first time ever in my life I've felt small," Heracles laughed, as he rowed out to sea in the giant cup, using an oar he had made from a tree trunk.

When he got to the island, he saw the scarlet cattle grazing on rolling red hills. There was an ugly, two-headed dog guarding them. It ran up to Heracles, snarling at him, but he simply swung his huge oar at the creature and knocked it five miles into the ocean.

Hearing the dog's pitiful yowl, Geryon came rushing over the hill. He was a monstrous figure, with three heads and bodies, and three sets of legs, all joined at the waist.

"What do you think you're doing?" said one of Geryon's heads.

"I'll kill you for that," said another.

The third leered as he scrabbled towards Heracles on all his legs, each arm brandishing a different weapon.

Heracles sighed. "I've fought a monster with hundreds of heads full of poisonous teeth," he said. "You don't bother me one bit." He whipped out his bow and shot Geryon straight through all three of his hearts with a single arrow.

Gathering the cattle, however, was a different matter. Just as he was rounding them up to load them into his golden cup boat, a gadfly came and began to bite their legs. They were so irritated by the insect that they started bellowing and kicking one another. Then they all charged off in different directions.

Heracles rounded them all up again, muttering crossly. But just as he was rounding the last bull into the herd, the gadfly struck again. The cattle scattered once more. "That two-headed mongrel could have been some use now, if only I hadn't belted it so far out to sea," grumbled Heracles as he went after them.

To make sure the cattle didn't run away a third time, he caught them two by two, tucking them under his arms and dropping them straight into the giant cup. Just as he crammed the last pair in, the two-headed dog finally made it back to the shore. It rushed at him, snapping at his heels, but Heracles launched the cup, leaped into it and rowed away across the ocean.

He didn't look back, and so he didn't see the goddess Hera appear on the shore of the island, scowling after him. The gadfly zoomed past her and, without taking her eyes off Heracles, she caught it in one hand. "Fat lot of good you did," she said to it, and crushed it to death in her fingers.

When Heracles herded the cattle into Eurystheus's palace garden, the king came out to greet him. "What would you like me to do with them?" Heracles asked.

"How about offering them as a gift to Hera?" suggested the king, and Heracles agreed.

High in the clouds, looking down, Hera watched as Heracles led all the beautiful red cattle to her temple, and left them there as an offering to her. She couldn't help but feel a little flattered. "Maybe you're not so bad after all, Heracles, son of Zeus," she admitted grudgingly.

XI
The golden apples

Heracles had been walking for so many days he'd lost count. King Eurystheus had ordered him to bring back three golden apples from the garden of the Hesperides. But finding the garden was proving more of a challenge than he'd expected. First, he'd had to wrestle a sea god to find out where it was. By the time he had him in a stranglehold, the directions were somewhat muffled, so all he knew was that the garden was close to Mount Atlas, somewhere near the edge of the world.

When at last he spotted a gigantic purple mountain on the horizon, he couldn't believe his luck. "That must be Mount Atlas," he said to himself, and he walked on with a spring in his step.

As he got nearer, Heracles realized that it wasn't a mountain at all, but an enormous giant. What he had taken for the rocky slopes were actually the giant's muscular legs, and the craggy cliffs he could see rising up into the sky were the giant's shoulders braced against the clouds.

As he reached the giant's feet, Heracles could just see his face through the clouds. It was purple with the strain of carrying the entire weight of the sky on his mountainous shoulders.

"Is your name Atlas?" Heracles called up.

"That's right," Atlas rumbled back.

"I've never met a giant before," said Heracles. "I thought you were a mountain. My name's Heracles."

"*The* Heracles?" Atlas asked incredulously, peering down through the clouds. "The one who wrestled the Nemean lion with his bare hands?"

"Yes," said Heracles.

"And killed the dreaded swamp beast, the many-headed hydra?" added the giant.

"That's me," Heracles replied.

"It's nice to meet you," Atlas boomed.

"I was wondering if you could help me," said Heracles.

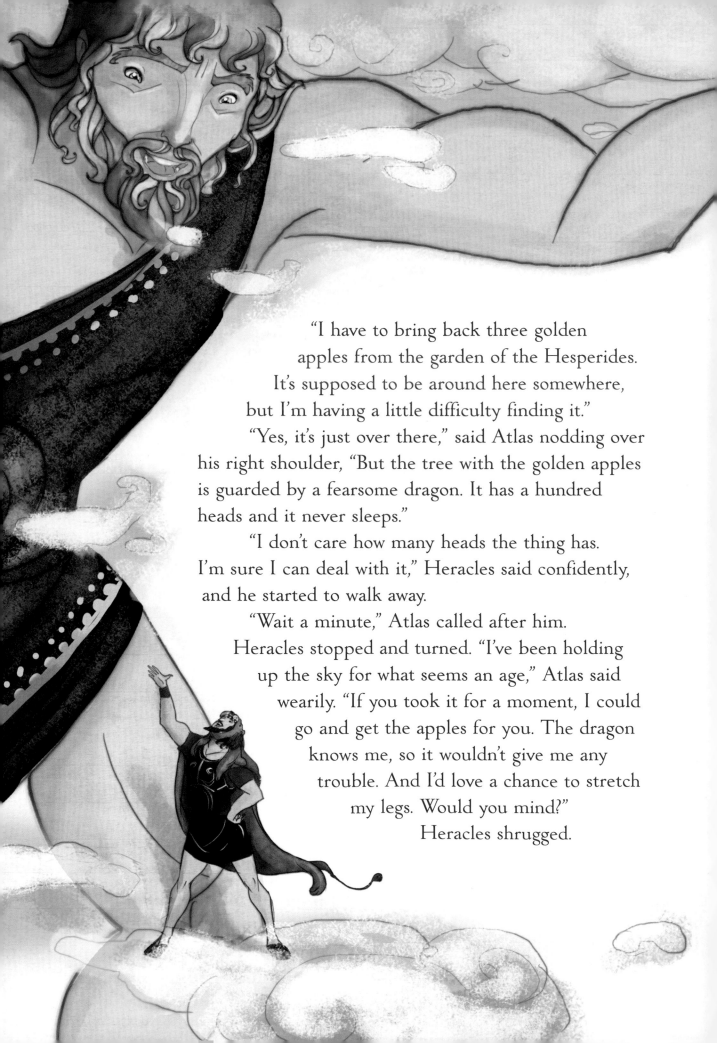

"I have to bring back three golden
apples from the garden of the Hesperides.
It's supposed to be around here somewhere,
but I'm having a little difficulty finding it."

"Yes, it's just over there," said Atlas nodding over
his right shoulder, "But the tree with the golden apples
is guarded by a fearsome dragon. It has a hundred
heads and it never sleeps."

"I don't care how many heads the thing has.
I'm sure I can deal with it," Heracles said confidently,
and he started to walk away.

"Wait a minute," Atlas called after him.
Heracles stopped and turned. "I've been holding
up the sky for what seems an age," Atlas said
wearily. "If you took it for a moment, I could
go and get the apples for you. The dragon
knows me, so it wouldn't give me any
trouble. And I'd love a chance to stretch
my legs. Would you mind?"

Heracles shrugged.

"No problem," he said. "I'd be happy to help out."
And he got himself ready to take the weight of the sky.

"Don't let it fall now," Atlas said anxiously. As he
heaved his burden onto Heracles's shoulders, there was
a rumble of thunder, a few clouds tumbled down in the
Sahara Desert and there was an unexpected hailstorm
over the city of Troy.

"I've got it," panted Heracles.

The sky was the heaviest thing he had ever held.
He had assumed that, being mostly made of air, it wouldn't
weigh much at all. But the clouds with all their raindrops
and bolts of lightning, the sun and the moon, not to
mention the heavens with all their stars, were so heavy that
his muscles bulged to twice their normal size and his legs
began to tremble.

Atlas stood upright and stretched luxuriously.
"That feels so good," he sighed.

"The golden apples," Heracles reminded him.
"You said you'd get them for me."

"Oh yes," said Atlas. "Of course," and he headed off
to the garden of the Hesperides.

As Heracles waited for Atlas to come back, the
sweat dripped from his brow. It ran down his chest and
created a river at his feet. He waited so long that he began
to wonder whether Atlas had fallen prey to the dragon
after all.

Heracles breathed a sigh of relief when the giant
finally returned, his arms full of shiny apples. But, instead

of taking back the sky, Atlas just stood there, arms crossed, looking down at him. There was a long pause, and Heracles could almost hear the cogs of the giant's ponderous mind working.

"You must be the only person apart from me who could possibly hold up the sky." Atlas said eventually. "I'm really sorry, friend, but I can't face taking it back, knowing I'd have to hold it for all eternity."

"I understand," Heracles answered calmly. "In fact, I don't mind at all."

Atlas's face brightened. "Really?" he said.

"Yes, of course," said Heracles. "The only thing is, if I'm going to hold up the sky for all eternity, then I could do with getting into a more comfortable position first. Would you mind taking it for just a minute while I rearrange myself?"

"No problem," said Atlas obligingly, and he put down the apples and braced his massive shoulders against the sky once more.

"Thanks," said Heracles, slipping out from under him. He gathered up the golden apples and set off back the way he had come.

"Where are you going?" called Atlas. "I thought we had a deal."

Heracles stopped and looked back. "What do you think I'm made of?" he laughed. "All muscles and no brain? It's your fate to hold up the sky, not mine. I'm taking these apples back to King Eurystheus, just as I promised him."

XII
Cerberus, the guard dog of the Underworld

"I think you have proved yourself to be a true hero," said King Eurystheus. "This last task will establish it beyond doubt. I want you to bring me Cerberus."

Heracles raised his eyebrows. "The dog that guards the land of the dead?"

"Yes," said the king. "Just bring it here to show me, and then you can take it back again."

Heracles shrugged, "Alright, why not?" he said. He was so strong now that not even the prospect of going into the land of the dead scared him. So he marched away to find an entrance to the Underworld.

The entrance he found was like the mouth of an ordinary cave, leading underground. But it was a cave that nobody else would have entered willingly. It seemed to suck light right into it and devour it until all that was left was a bone-chilling darkness. Heracles felt his way inside the cave and began to descend into the bowels of the earth. Muffled shrieks and moans of dead people's spirits floated up from below.

As he went deeper and deeper, he caught sight of a few dead souls. They drifted up to him, their ghostly bodies barely visible in the gloom.

"Give us your blood, mortal," they hissed, "we need it to feel whole again." But when they saw who it was their eyes widened and they fled from Heracles, wailing in fear.

Heracles quickened his pace. In front of him, he saw the glimmer of the River Styx. On the other side was the Underworld. It seemed to glow, not with the vibrant sunshine that bathed the earth's surface, but with an eerie half-light that made everything look faded and pale.

Heracles watched more souls drift along the sludgy banks of the river and crowd at the ferry landing to ask the ferryman, Charon, to take them across.

"You can't cross yet, your body hasn't been buried," Charon snarled at one pale sailor. "I'm not taking you if you can't pay the fare," he said to another. An ancient-looking woman pushed forward and pressed a coin into his outstretched hand, and he stood aside to let her climb on board.

As Heracles neared the boat, Charon looked up, "As for you, you've no business here at all," he growled at Heracles. "You're clearly still alive."

"I've been sent here to take Cerberus for a walk," Heracles told him casually. Before Charon could protest, he pushed a coin into his palm and stepped onto the ferry. His enormous weight made the boat sink considerably in the water, and the ghostly woman passenger leaped back onto the shore. "You can come back for me," she said hurriedly to Charon, glancing nervously at the murky river, which was swimming with translucent spirits of dead sea monsters.

It's not surprising Charon was such a gloomy character. His father was the god of darkness and his mother was the goddess of night. She rode in her chariot, drawing the veil of darkness across the sky at the end of every day.

94

Charon took up his oars and began to row Heracles across the river. "I don't know why people like you meddle with the Underworld before their time," he grumbled. He drew the boat up to the landing stage, and Heracles jumped off, saying, "I'll be back shortly with Cerberus."

But before Heracles could go any further, there was a strange rumble and a beautiful, pale goddess appeared before him. It was Persephone, queen of the Underworld.

"You must be Heracles," she said. "The monsters you have slain have passed this way and told us all about your amazing strength. But what brings you down here to the land of the dead?"

Heracles bowed his head respectfully, "Persephone," he said, "I hope, with your blessing, to borrow Cerberus."

"What do you want to do with him?" the goddess asked curiously.

"I just have to show him to King Eurystheus, who has set me the task. Then I can bring him back again," Heracles replied.

Persephone looked him up and down and said, "I don't see why I should stop you. Please come this way."

She led him to the gates of the Underworld, where a monstrous, snarling dog was standing guard. It had a writhing serpent for a tail and three huge heads, each baring an impressive set of teeth. But as soon as this vicious-looking creature caught sight of Heracles, it cowered and began to whimper like a puppy.

"It seems even Cerberus has heard about your monster-killing exploits," said Persephone dryly.

Heracles took off his belt and wrapped it around one of the creature's heads like a leash. "I promise I'll return him within a day," he said bowing to the queen.

Persephone shrugged. "Days have no meaning here, but I trust you to bring him back."

Heracles thanked her, and walked back to the riverbank with Cerberus at his heels. Souls coming off the ferry parted around him, trembling at the sight of the world's strongest man leading the dreaded guard dog of the Underworld.

"Keep that hideous creature away from me," Charon grumbled nervously, as Heracles dragged Cerberus onto the ferry. The boat rocked under their great weight, and water slopped in over the sides.

Charon rowed them back across the River Styx, complaining all the way. Then Heracles made his way back above ground to daylight. With a firm grip on the belt leash, he returned to Eurystheus's palace and presented Cerberus to the king.

"Congratulations, Heracles," the king said, keeping his distance from the beast. He was impressed by Heracles's bravery, and more than a little relieved this was the last monstrous creature the hero would be bringing into the palace. "You have completed all the tasks," the king continued. "Once you have returned this beast to its rightful place, you will be free to go. You have shown yourself to be a true hero."

Heracles bowed deeply before him and took his leave for the very last time.

High in the clouds above Mount Olympus, Hera watched Heracles set off into the world a free man. Zeus peered over her shoulder and said, "There goes my son. What do you think of him now?"

"I hate to admit it," sighed Hera, "but he truly is a god among men. I can't bring myself to hate him any more. He's proven himself once and for all."

"I'm glad you think so," said Zeus. "Because I've been thinking – he's half god and half man, but when his human half dies, I would like to offer him a place up here with us. It's where he belongs."

Hera smiled. If Heracles became a god, then there would be no human part left in him, and nothing to be jealous about. "That suits me fine," she said.

The minotaur and the labyrinth

When Queen Pasiphae of Crete gave birth, the midwife's scream of horror echoed all around the palace. Even days later, she couldn't bring herself to describe what she'd seen. "It wasn't human," was the only thing she would say.

The queen herself stayed in her rooms and would speak to nobody. King Minos took charge. The only person he allowed into the nursery was a strong male servant. Not even Ariadne, his own daughter, was permitted to visit.

Ariadne didn't dare disobey her father, but she burned with curiosity. Over the weeks following the birth, she heard all kinds of strange noises coming from the nursery — snorts, snarls and thundering footsteps — and they didn't sound as if they came from a baby.

As the months went by, the thumps and growls grew louder, and on more than one occasion the servant staggered from the room bleeding as though he'd been gored by a bull. "Please tell me what's in there," Ariadne begged him.

"Your father said he'd kill me if I said a word," the man replied.

"He probably meant it too," thought Ariadne. Her father was a ruthless man. She didn't press the servant any further. At any rate, his face had told her all she needed to know. It was no child in that room; it was a monster.

Then one day, she heard a terrible commotion, ending in a blood-curdling scream, and the servant didn't come out of the nursery at all. The monster had eaten him alive.

That afternoon, the king went to see Daedalus, his chief inventor. "I need you to create a place where I can hide a minotaur," he said.

"A mino-what?" asked Daedalus.

"Never you mind," snapped the king. "A creature that must never escape. Build me a prison to contain it!"

Daedalus set to work immediately, and came up with a brilliant design for a maze of tunnels beneath the palace. Under his close supervision, a team of builders began work on it right away.

The maze was so complicated that nobody who entered it would ever be able to find their way out. In fact, when one of the workmen ventured back into the tunnels

Daedalus was famous for inventing all kinds of wonderful things, from the very first sails on ships to a musical floor for Ariadne to dance on when she was a little girl.

to pick up a chisel he'd left behind, he was never seen again.

Daedalus called his maze the labyrinth. With the help of the king's army, the minotaur was driven into it, and the huge iron door at the entrance was bolted shut. For the first few days, the creature could be heard snorting angrily and ramming the door. But it soon wandered off into the labyrinth. The noise grew less and less distinct until nothing could be heard but the occasional faint bellow.

"I suppose at least we're safe now," Ariadne said to her father.

"Yes, we are," said the king. He flashed her a dark look. "But I've been thinking – maybe my monstrous prisoner could be more useful than I thought..." He told her he had written a letter to his enemies in Athens demanding that they send seven young men and seven young women to be fed to the minotaur. If they refused to sacrifice these few, he had threatened to slaughter everyone in the city. "That should keep them in check," he gloated.

Ariadne felt sick. "How can you be my father?" she said in disgust. "You're more of a monster than the one you've locked up." But the king just laughed and waved her away.

A few days later, the fourteen terrified victims arrived. They were pushed into the labyrinth with the king looking on. "There's a way out on the other side," he lied cruelly. "If you find your way through, you may go home."

The poor prisoners ran as fast as they could into the gloom. During the next few weeks, their cries were heard echoing over the island as the minotaur found and devoured every last one of them.

The following year, King Minos demanded another fourteen victims, and again the third year running. Ariadne watched as they were led in to the palace, wishing there was something she could do to save them.

As the prisoners trudged past, one of them caught her father's eye. "Stop!" he ordered, staring closely at the man. "Aren't you Theseus, Prince of Athens?"

"That's right," Theseus replied coolly. "I've come to slay the minotaur."

"Oh really?" the king mocked. "Then we will allow the beast a decent last meal before you slay it. You can face him alone tomorrow." He had Theseus flung into jail overnight, while the other prisoners were pushed into the labyrinth there and then.

In desperation, Ariadne went to see Daedalus. "You invented the labyrinth," she said, "which makes you partly responsible. You have to help me put a stop to this."

Old Daedalus had known Ariadne all her life, and her words filled him with shame. "What do you need me to do?" he asked.

"Tell me how the last prisoner can find his way out of the labyrinth," said Ariadne. "He means to slay the monster, and I think he may well live to tell the tale."

Daedalus thought for a moment. Then he went into his workshop and brought out a large ball of thin, golden thread. "Tell him to unwind this as he goes along," he said. "Then he can follow the thread to find his way out of the labyrinth."

Ariadne thanked him and hurried away.

She found Theseus sitting calmly in his prison cell.
He looked up as she slipped in through the door, and the
determination in his eyes made her heart leap with hope.
"I've brought this to help you," she said. She handed him
the ball of thread and told him what to do. "I'll pray to
the gods that you succeed."

"Thank you," said Theseus. "It seems not everyone
in this kingdom is a monster."

Ariadne turned to go, but then she paused. "I can't
stay here after what my father has done," she said. "When
you come out of the labyrinth tomorrow, I'll be waiting.
Can I escape with you?"

"Certainly," said Theseus.

The next day, Theseus entered the labyrinth.
He strode into the gloom, unwinding the ball of thread as
he went. The tunnels seemed to go on forever, twisting and
turning this way and that. Before long he had completely
lost his sense of direction.

Impatient to confront the minotaur, Theseus stopped
every few hundred paces and shouted, "Monster, are you
there?" He listened carefully for a reply, but all he heard
was his own voice echoing eerily around the tunnels.

The tenth time he shouted, a fearful voice called
back, "Theseus, is that you?" Out of the darkness crept
the thirteen prisoners who had been sent into the labyrinth
the night before.

Before Theseus had time to reply, a ferocious bellow
filled the air. Something was approaching from behind.
The prisoners fled, and Theseus turned to face the minotaur.

All he saw was a pair of eyes
burning red in the darkness, and then
suddenly the minotaur was upon him.
It seemed to fill the entire tunnel as it
charged — a hulking mass with two massive,
sharp horns heading right for him.
He dived clear just in time, landing
in a tumbled heap on the ground.
The beast turned, snorting
wildly, and that was when Theseus
saw it clearly for the first time.
It had the body of a man, and the
head of a bull, and the eyes of
a blood-thirsty monster.

No sooner had he scrambled to his feet than the minotaur was upon him again. Theseus swung his sword but it glanced off one of the beast's horns. The horn drove into his arm, slashing it open.

Gasping with pain, Theseus thrust his blade again as the minotaur thundered past. His sword caught the beast's shoulder as it spun around to face him, and drew blood. The enraged creature roared and barged into Theseus, knocking him to the ground.

Theseus rolled out of the way of its horns just before they ran him through. He leaped to his feet as the minotaur tried once more to gore him, and its horns skewered the wall of the tunnel instead. Stone crumbled from the wall under the force of the blow. Grunting with frustration, the beast wrenched its horns free, as Theseus lunged at it. This time, he succeeded in driving his blade into the minotaur's shoulder. The beast arched its back and bellowed in pain. Theseus retreated down the tunnel and awaited his chance.

The minotaur eyed him, snorting heavily. Then it lowered its head and charged. Theseus steeled himself until the very last second, then he slammed his back to the side of the tunnel, gripped his sword in both hands and thrust it out in front of him. The charging beast ran straight into the outstretched blade, stumbled and fell to the ground.

Theseus stood over it and plunged his blade deep into its chest. The minotaur gave one last, hoarse bellow. The light in its eyes faded, and it was dead.

Theseus sheathed his sword, and a ragged cheer met his ears. He turned to find the thirteen other Athenians gazing at him in awe.

"That was amazing," said one.

"Incredible," another joined in.

A young woman burst into tears. "But we're doomed to die anyway," she wailed miserably. "How will we ever find our way out of this place?"

Theseus looked around by his feet until he saw the end of the golden thread glinting in the gloom. "Like this," he said. He picked up the thread and followed it, winding it up as he went. It led them all the way back along the twisting, turning tunnels to freedom.

Ariadne was waiting at the entrance of the labyrinth, silhouetted against the early morning sun. She had bribed the gatekeeper to abandon his post for the morning, and had everything prepared for a speedy escape. "There's a ship waiting for us in the port," she whispered. "Hurry before my father notices I'm gone."

They ran from the palace and down through the barely-awake city to the port.

Out on the sparkling, turquoise sea, Ariadne stood on the bow of the ship and watched her homeland fade into the distance. She smiled and turned to watch as the Athenians lifted Theseus onto their shoulders and cheered. They hailed him as a hero and promised that the story of how he had slain the minotaur and saved their lives would be told forever more.

On the way back from Crete, Theseus left Ariadne sleeping on the island of Naxos, where Dionysus, the god of wine, fell in love with her and made her his wife.

Daphne, the girl who turned into a tree

Daphne was a beautiful nymph. She was the daughter of a river god and had smooth, lily-white skin, sparkling eyes and moved with a fluid grace that enchanted all who laid eyes on her.

She grew up in a forest, on the banks of her father's river. She spent her time swimming in the flowing water and wandering happily through the trees in the company of the timid animals that lived there.

One day, a man walking through the forest came across her as she sat by the river. Daphne had never seen a man before, and she was curious about him.

He stopped and stared at her, and when she smiled, he blurted. "You're the most beautiful girl I've ever met."

Daphne shrugged. "You're the only man I've ever met," she answered.

"How can I win your heart?" the man asked her.

Daphne's smiled turned into a worried frown. "I don't know what you mean," she said. "My heart isn't a thing that can be won like a trophy."

"Come, come," the man insisted, taking her arm. "There must be some way I can make you mine."

"There isn't," said Daphne, horrified at the very thought of being owned. She got to her feet, brushed the man's hand away and ran off into the trees.

Her next encounter with a man went the same way, and the next was no better. It seemed that all men wanted was to possess her – an idea she didn't like one bit. She decided to keep away from them in the future.

When she told her father of her decision, he looked worried. "You shouldn't root yourself so firmly in one view," he advised her. "You're still so young. You don't even know what it is to fall in love yet. One day you might meet someone to whom you actually want to belong – and who you want to belong to you."

"Please don't say that, Father," said Daphne. "All I want is to be left in peace."

Some time later, one sunny afternoon, the young god Apollo was wandering through the forest, when he caught sight of Daphne through the trees. His heart leaped at the sight of her. "Hello," he said.

To his surprise, the girl hurried away without even a glance in his direction.

Apollo ran after her. "Excuse me, won't you please stop a moment?" he called.

"Go away," Daphne retorted. "I'm not interested."

"But you don't even know what I want yet," Apollo said in surprise. "You haven't even looked at me."

Indeed, if Daphne had taken the time to glance back, perhaps it would have been a different story. Apollo was astoundingly good-looking. He was tall and strong, with a crown of unruly golden curls and a warm smile.

But Daphne had made up her mind. "You're all the same," she shouted. "You like what you see and so you want to own me. You don't even know me."

"No," agreed Apollo, "but I'd like to. Please wait. I don't think I can be like the others, whoever they are. I'm a god, for a start —"

Daphne laughed disbelievingly and broke into a run.

"Really, I am," insisted Apollo, trying to keep up with her. "My name's Apollo. I'm the god of healing, of sunlight, of music. I do think you're beautiful, but I only want to talk to you."

But Daphne just ran even faster. She wove this way and that through the trees, her silken hair flowing behind her like a river. But try as she might to lose her pursuer, she could always hear his footsteps behind her.

"If he really is a god," she thought in panic, "then he has the power to catch me, whether I like it or not." She ran and ran until her lungs were bursting and her muscles burned. Then, just when she felt she could run no further, she heard the whisper of the river ahead. "Father," she cried out, "if you have any power over nature at all, change me into something to stop men bothering me!"

The whisper of the water became a roar, and right away Daphne felt her legs grow heavy. She looked down to see that her feet had become tree roots, planted firmly in the ground, and rings of bark were creeping up and around her waist.

Hearing a gasp behind her, she turned and saw her pursuer for the very first time. Apollo had stopped a few feet away and was staring at her, his honest face filled with horror. "What have you done?" he whispered.

Daphne gazed back at him in silence as the bark rose around her chest. Then, just as the wood grain began to creep across her soft, white throat, she suddenly stretched out her arms to Apollo. But before his fingertips could touch hers, her arms had become branches and her fingers leaves, fluttering in the breeze.

Moments later, the transformation was complete. All that remained of the beautiful nymph was her grace, as her branches swayed gently in the breeze.

Daphne had become a laurel tree.

Apollo looked sadly at the laurel tree. He laid his hand on its trunk and thought he felt the flutter of a heartbeat through the bark. He pressed his lips to it, but felt it shrink away beneath them.

"You will never be mine," he said, taking a step away from the tree. "And I respect your decision. But with your consent, I'd like to wear a wreath of your leaves as a crown." The upper branches of the laurel tree moved gently, as if nodding in agreement.

Following Apollo's example, all the Greek gods started to wear laurel crowns, and they awarded them to people as a mark of great respect.

Jason
and the
golden fleece

When a tall stranger turned up at the palace, King Pelias felt uneasy. Not only did the young man look surprisingly familiar, but he marched right up to the throne as if he owned it. Yet it was something else that really bothered the king.

"Why are you only wearing one sandal? Where's the other one?" he asked suspiciously, before the stranger had time to say a word.

The stranger looked down at his bare foot. "I lost it giving an old woman a lift across a river," he answered.

Pelias shifted uncomfortably on his throne. Many years before, the goddess Hera had warned him that his downfall would come from a man who had lost a sandal in exactly this way. It had seemed ridiculous at the time, but now he was worried.

"Anyway, to come straight to the point," said the stranger. "I'm your nephew, Jason. I've come to claim my rightful place as king."

A wave of shock rippled around the court. "Whatever do you mean?" spluttered the king. "For a start, I don't have a nephew."

"Allow me to explain," Jason said. "When you stole the throne from my father, he was already old and frail so he didn't dare challenge you. Then, I was born. He feared for my life, knowing you to be a ruthless man, so he smuggled me away to be brought up in hiding."

People began to eye the king suspiciously.

"Anyway, now I'm old enough," Jason continued, "and my father is dead, I've come to claim my kingdom."

Beads of sweat appeared on Pelias's forehead. It was going to be hard to get out of this one. The boy was the image of his father, and everything he said was true. He stared at his nephew in silence, wracking his brains for a solution. Finally he spoke up. "I wouldn't want to entrust the kingdom to someone with no experience," he said slowly. "If you are worthy of ruling, I presume you'll have no objection to proving it?"

"None at all," said Jason.

"Then bring me the famous golden fleece from the kingdom of Colchis," the king said, "and I'll gladly give up the throne."

"Very well," Jason agreed. "I will."

Pelias sank back in relief as he watched his nephew leave. Colchis was far away across the sea, and any voyage there would be dangerous and difficult. Even if Jason managed to get there, the golden fleece would not be easy to win. The king did not expect Jason to return.

Jason began to prepare for the journey immediately. He went to the best shipbuilder he could find and asked him to build a sturdy ship that could sail as fast as the wind. Then he set about gathering a crew.

He found ready support for his cause. Many older people remembered his father, and those who didn't, warmed to Jason's straightforward, energetic nature. News of his quest spread quickly. By the time his ship was ready, Jason had a crew of fifty of the bravest men and women in the land.

They sailed for many months, on rough seas and on smooth; through fierce storms and under the glare of the beating sun. When all their food was gone, they managed to live off whatever fish they could catch in the sea.

Then, at last, a small island appeared on the horizon. "Let's stop there and stock up on supplies," said Jason.

They drew into the rocky bay, and a large palace came into view. Jason decided at once to investigate. Zetes and Calais, winged twins, went with him.

As they walked, a terrible stench filled the air. It became more and more unbearable the closer they got to the palace. Burying their noses in their cloaks, they pressed on. Close up, the palace looked empty and neglected. There were holes in the roof, and some feeble attempts had been made to cover some of the windows with wooden boards, but they were all split and broken. Cautiously, Jason and the twins pushed open a heavy door that was hanging off its hinges and went inside.

Jason named his ship the *Argo*, which means 'swift'. His crew became known as the Argonauts, and they were a lively bunch...

Orpheus, whose beautiful music could whip up a sailing wind or calm the seas...

Zetes and Calais, the winged twin sons of the North Wind...

and Atalanta, a fearless female warrior who had been brought up by bears.

117

Harpies were foul creatures. Their name means 'snatchers', and they were known for snatching things – or even people – and carrying them away.

Sitting alone at a long table strewn with the rotten, stinking remains of a meal was a thin old man. He looked up as they approached, but his eyes were white and blind. "Who goes there?" he asked in a wavering voice.

"A friend," Jason replied gently.

"Ah, Jason," said the man. "I was hoping you'd be here soon."

"How do you know who I am?" Jason asked, stunned.

"I may be blind," the man replied, "but I have other ways of seeing. My name is Phineus."

"I've heard of you. People say you can see into the future..." Jason said. "If that's true, please could you tell me whether I will win the golden fleece?"

Phineus shook his head. "Look at the mess I'm in," he said. "The gods hated me telling people what would happen. They blinded me as punishment and sent harpies to torment me."

Jason was about to ask what a harpy was, when a servant came in carrying a plate piled high with bread and olives, figs and apricots. He laid it down on the table and scurried back out of the room. Immediately, the sound of beating wings filled the air and three revolting, vulture-like creatures burst in through the windows. Jason caught a glimpse of their leering human faces as they seized some of the food in their filthy claws, and flew back outside. The stench they left behind turned his stomach, and all the food left on Phineus's plate was seeping and rotten.

Phineus sighed. "I haven't had a decent meal in months. What a pathetic king I am. Nobody can bear

118

to live here. I've only one servant left. I've paid him everything I own to stay with me."

The servant poked his head around the door. "Shall I try again?" he asked.

Phineus nodded. "Sometimes you can get a quick mouthful," he explained to Jason, "before they come."

The servant hurried back with another plate of food. The harpies circled outside, cackling viciously.

Jason stepped forward. "Eat, Phineus," he urged, his hand on his sword. "I'll kill them if they come near."

"You won't catch them," Phineus said. But he reached for a piece of bread nonetheless.

The harpies dived into the room again, claws outstretched. Jason drove them off, but they dodged his blade and gathered to dive again.

In one fluid motion, Zetes and Calais spread their wings and took to the air with their swords drawn. The harpies veered away and out of the window, screeching in surprise. They were speedy, but the twins were as swift as the wind. The brothers gave chase, and soon they had all disappeared from view.

Phineus ate hungrily. "Your friends will be back soon," he said between mouthfuls. "Meanwhile, in return for your kindness, I will tell you something you need to know. There's danger ahead. Your route is about to take you through the Clashing Rocks. Every ship that has ever tried to sail through them has been smashed to smithereens. But if you do what I tell you, you'll have a slim chance of making it."

By the time the twins had returned, Phineus had finished his first meal in months and Jason was sitting beside him holding a caged dove on his knee.

"We caught them," panted Zetes, sheathing his sword with a flourish. "They'll never bother you again."

Phineus smiled, "May the gods reward your kindness with a safe voyage," he said.

With the old man's blessing, and plenty of fresh provisions, Jason and the twins returned to the rest of the crew and they set sail once more.

Before long, they came to a narrow channel of water, enclosed on both sides by towering cliffs. The only way forward was to sail right through the middle.

When the ship drew close to the opening, Jason said, "Hold it here." Then he released the dove into the air. "Phineus said that if this dove makes it through the rocks alive, we have a chance of doing the same. Get ready to follow it when I give the word."

Everyone watched as the bird flew between the rocks. There was a shudder and a groan, and to their horror the cliffs on either side started to move. Like two massive fists, they started to come together, churning the sea up into foam. Their shadows swallowed up the bird's tiny form. They got closer and closer until they collided with a thundering crash that almost split the sky in two.

Then the cliffs began to move apart again, and two white feathers fluttered down onto the water. The crew's hearts sank. Then they caught sight of the dove flying beyond the rocks. It had made it through alive.

"Now!" yelled
Jason. "Row like you've
never rowed before. Our
lives depend on it!" Everyone
began straining at the oars and the
ship surged into the narrow passage.
The rocks continued to move slowly
apart until they had returned to their
original position. But before the ship
was even halfway through, they started
lurching closer together again.

Huge waves crashed over the deck, drenching everyone to the skin. Gasping for air, they kept on rowing. The rocks moved ever closer, casting bone-chilling shadows across the deck. At any minute, the crew would be crushed to death.

"Keep going!" cried Jason, heaving at the oars.

The ship was just squeezing out of the other side when the rocks closed in on its stern. The wood began to splinter as they squeezed tighter and tighter, and the crew strained at the oars with all their might. Then with a grinding crunch, the ship burst free — just as the rocks crashed together. Only the very tip of the stern was lost. The rocks drew slowly back, and the crew dropped their oars and sank onto the deck exhausted.

When they'd recovered their strength, they sailed on to Colchis. The sun was beginning to glow red over the sea when they finally put down anchor in the bustling port and made their way to the palace.

Jason asked to see the king. "I've come to claim the golden fleece," he told him.

The king frowned. "Young fools always come here thinking they can win my golden fleece," he said, "and every one of them dies trying. It's guarded by a dragon that never sleeps."

"I'll fight the dragon," said Jason, undeterred.

"Before you get to the dragon, you must complete two tasks," the king said grudgingly.

A young woman with jet-black hair and glittering green eyes put her hand on the king's arm. "Father, it's late," she said in a voice as smooth as honey. "Why don't we wait until tomorrow? There will be more people here then to witness this young fool's defeat."

The king nodded, looking pleased with the idea.

"I'll show you to a room where you can rest," said the woman, and she led Jason and his crew out of the hall. "I can help you," she whispered when they were out of earshot. "The tasks are impossible without my magic."

Jason was completely taken aback. "Why would you help me win something from your own father?" he asked.

She fixed him with a bewitching stare and said, "Because you're the man I want to marry."

Jason's skin tingled under her gaze. "I don't even know your name," he said.

"Medea," the woman answered. She took Jason's hand and led him to her room. There, she prepared a magic ointment made from all kinds of strange ingredients, and gave it to him in a little jar. "Rub this on your skin," she said. "It will protect you. But beware — you'll still need all your strength and wits to survive."

In the morning, Jason and his crew were taken to a field outside the palace, where a crowd had gathered to watch. "The first task," announced the king, "is to put a yoke on these bulls and drive them across this field."

It sounded simple enough, but as Jason approached the two hulking creatures, flames came streaming from their nostrils. These were clearly no ordinary bulls. Jason kept on edging towards them, and the crowd gasped as he was engulfed in the fire. But Medea's potion was so powerful that, whereas anyone else would have been burned to cinders, Jason was only slightly singed.

Jason was filled with relief. The potion worked; he had nothing to fear. Confidently he walked straight up to the bulls and took hold of their horns. After a few disgruntled snorts, the beasts calmed down. Jason harnessed the bulls and drove them up and down the field as though they were ordinary farm animals.

He had dug up half the field before the king growled, "That's enough!" He didn't look at all pleased. "Now plant these dragons' teeth," he said curtly, and handed Jason a pouch full of yellow, pointed teeth.

Jason looked at them curiously, wondering what purpose planting dragons' teeth seeds could possibly serve. Then he shrugged and sprinkled them into the soil. Immediately, four identical, fully-armed warriors sprang up from the ground. They advanced on him murderously, fresh soil falling from their limbs.

Jason drew his sword and his crew sprang forward to defend him, but the king held up his hand. "He has to fight them by himself, or else he forfeits the golden fleece," he warned. Reluctantly, they fell back.

As Jason clashed swords with the warriors, another two sprouted from the soil and attacked him from behind. He dodged blows from the first four and whirled around to fight the second pair.

Another warrior emerged and joined the battle, and then another and another, until Jason could barely be seen through the forest of slashing swords.

Jason fought fast and furiously, but nothing seemed to stop the soil-grown army. When he lopped an arm off one warrior, it simply picked up the sword in its other hand and kept on fighting doggedly as if nothing had happened.

To gain a few seconds' breathing space, he thrust a couple of warriors away from him. They toppled into the warriors behind, knocking them over. Exhausted, Jason raised his sword again as they got to their feet. But instead of attacking him, the fallen warriors turned on the ones that had knocked them over.

Suddenly Jason realized what he must do.

He picked up a rock and hurled it into the midst of another group of warriors. It sent them into confusion. They all looked around to see which one of them had thrown the rock, and then set upon one another with their swords.

"It works!" Jason exclaimed. He threw another rock into a different band of warriors, who turned on one another too. Soon they were all fighting among themselves, and seemed to have forgotten all about him.

The king was furious. "Enough!" he shouted. But the warriors paid no attention. They kept on hacking away at one another, lopping off heads and chopping off limbs until they had nothing left to hold their swords with. Only then did they fall to the ground, defeated.

"Shall I fight the dragon next?" Jason asked, his spirit entirely undampened.

The king glared at him. "That can wait until tomorrow," he snapped. "I'll have some food and wine brought to your rooms." Then he turned his back and walked away.

That evening, Jason and his crew were just about to start drinking the wine, when Medea rushed in.

"Don't drink that," she cried, wrenching the jug from an indignant sailor's hand. "It's got enough sleeping powder in it to knock out an entire army. My father doesn't want to give up his precious golden fleece," she explained. "He told me he's going to have you all murdered in your sleep tonight. You must escape at once."

"I'm not leaving without the fleece," Jason told her.

"Then we'll have to get it now," Medea answered.

Jason took the jug of drugged wine from her hand and a bowl from the table, and they followed Medea out of the palace. She took them to a grove of trees where, draped over a branch of an oak tree was the golden fleece. It truly lived up to its name. It gleamed bright gold even in the dead of night.

Curled around the trunk of the tree lay a fearsome dragon. Its skin looked like green metal, and each of its jet-black talons was as long as a man's forearm. Its watchful eyes glittered dangerously as Jason and Medea approached.

Jason poured the drugged wine into the bowl he'd brought from their room and began to push it slowly closer to the beast. "This may help you sleep," he whispered.

The creature watched him without blinking. Before Jason got anywhere near, it raised its head and blasted a huge stream of flames at him. Despite Medea's magic lotion, Jason winced with pain as the fire scorched his skin.

Just then, he heard a low, rhythmic murmur behind him, as the bowl shifted. He watched in fascination as it moved out of his hands and slid all by itself along the ground to the dragon.

Jason glanced back at Medea. She was staring concentratedly at the bowl, her lips mouthing some kind of spell. When it reached the dragon's feet, the bowl stopped. The beast sniffed it suspiciously, then dipped its nose inside and lapped up a little wine. Steam hissed from the sides of its mouth as the liquid quenched the fire in the creature's throat. It drank deeply until all the wine was gone.

Almost immediately, its eyelids began to droop. It shook its head, looking confused, and stared around hazily. Slowly its head sank lower and lower, until at last, it laid it on the ground and closed its yellow eyes.

Quietly, Jason got to his feet and crept towards the tree. He was just reaching over the dragon's head to lift the fleece from the branch, when the beast shifted. Jason froze, his hand on the hilt of his sword. But the dragon just gave a heavy sigh and then began to snore.

Jason reached up again and slid the fleece carefully off the branch. Then he crept back to his waiting friends, and they all hurried down to their ship.

They set sail at once, taking Medea and the golden fleece with them. The wind was on their side and they sped across the ink-dark waves. By the time the king's soldiers came with glinting swords to their beds, Jason and his crew were long gone.

When Jason returned home and presented King Pelias with the golden fleece, the king couldn't help but let out a groan. Now there was absolutely no denying Jason's right to the throne.

The golden fleece came from a winged ram, which was sacrificed to the gods and became the constellation Aries.

Icarus, the boy who flew too high

Icarus paced around the tiny room for the thousandth time. "I'm bored," he complained. "King Minos can't possibly keep us locked up here forever, can he?"

"He could do far worse than that," answered his father, Daedalus. "I helped his enemy, Theseus, escape. It's a crime punishable by death. The only reason he hasn't had us killed already is that I'm far too useful to him alive."

Sighing, he bent over his clay tablet and continued to work on his new design for a bridge. As long as he continued to produce ground-breaking inventions, the king would spare them. But it was a terrible burden knowing that both of their lives depended on the success of his latest idea.

"Why did he have to lock me up as well?" Icarus muttered sulkily. "I could be plotting your escape by now."

Daedalus didn't look up from his work. "I imagine that's exactly why he locked you up, Son."

Icarus slumped onto his elbows on the window ledge, startling a couple of doves into flight. He stared at them enviously. Picking up a stray feather and stroking it idly against his cheek, he murmured, "If only we could fly, we could escape from this tower and go wherever we wanted."

"That's it!" Daedalus exclaimed, flinging down his tablet. "You've hit the nail right on the head!"

"Whatever do you mean?" asked Icarus.

"It's simple: I'll make us wings and we'll fly away," said Daedalus, already scratching busily at a fresh tablet. Within an hour, he'd come up with a rough design for human-sized wings. "That's the easy part," he said. "Now we have to collect enough feathers to actually make the things."

From that moment on, they gave half their tiny daily ration of bread to the birds. More and more birds flocked to the little tower, eager to be fed, and each day Icarus collected the stray feathers they left behind and hid them under his straw mattress.

After a few months, they had so many feathers the mattress would barely stay on the floor. Icarus and his father had grown quite thin from their reduced rations.

"The lighter we are the better," joked Daedalus. "Still, before we waste away entirely, I'd better get on with making those wings."

He reached out of the window of the tower and pulled some vines from the wall. After stripping them of leaves, he wove the supple stems into four large frames. Next, he collected all the wax that he used for making design models and laid it in the sunshine to soften it. He dotted the softened, sticky wax along the frames and pushed feather after feather into it.

Daedalus had studied the birds carefully over the last few months, and modified his design according to what he learned. He made sure that each feather overlapped the last, and lined them up in order of size to look just like a real bird's wings.

Icarus watched in fascination as the wings took shape. When they were finally ready, he ran his fingers over the soft feathers and glanced at the sky. "Do you really think they'll work?" he asked.

"Have any of my inventions ever failed?" Daedalus replied. He lifted one pair of wings onto his son's shoulders and tied them on.

Icarus raised his arms and flapped them cautiously. To his delight, his feet left the floor and he hovered in the air for a moment before dropping gently down again.

Icarus scrambled eagerly onto the window ledge. Looking down, he could see all the way to the foot of the tower. It was a dizzying sight. But then he turned his gaze to the sparkling sea and the vast, empty sky above, and felt excitement rising again in his chest.

Icarus took a deep breath, spread his wings
and leaped into the air. The wind caught him straight
away, and he glided smoothly out above the sea. The air
rushed past, ruffling his hair, and a broad grin spread
across his face. Flying was incredible.

A shadow fell over him as his father flew overhead.
"Careful now," he said. "Don't fly too low in case the sea spray
dampens your feathers; and don't fly too high in case the
sun melts the wax. Just follow right behind me."

135

Flapping his wings steadily, Daedalus took the lead and Icarus followed him obediently. Far, far below, farmers were working in a patchwork of fields. Icarus was fascinated by how small everything looked: tiny sheep grazed in tiny meadows, tended by toy shepherds. Before he knew it, they were gliding past craggy cliffs and out over the open sea.

A lone fisherman looked up as they passed, and dropped his net when he saw the winged figures soaring across the sky. "They must be gods," he whispered in awe, and counted himself lucky to have caught a glimpse.

Icarus certainly felt superhuman. He was so used to flying now that it was as if he'd been doing it all his life, and he was growing mighty bored of looking at the soles of his father's dusty old sandals. It was high time for a bit of fun. He swooped down to the sea and skimmed low over the glittering waves, so low that he could see jade-green turtles and schools of silvery fish swimming beneath the surface.

Then he flapped his wings and climbed higher and higher into the sky, until even the birds were beneath him and the sky was his alone.

His father's voice came floating up from beneath him. "Icarus, come down at once!"

Frowning, Icarus flapped his wings and flew even higher. "Why shouldn't I enjoy myself?" he grumbled, squinting down at his father, who by now was so far below him he looked no bigger than a sparrow.

The light on the sea was so dazzling, Icarus
shut his eyes. "Free at last," he thought, as he soared
closer and closer to the sun.

He didn't realize that the sun's hot rays were melting
the wax in his wings; he didn't see the feathers dropping
out one by one.

But Daedalus did. When feathers from his son's
wings began to flutter down, he shouted himself hoarse
trying to warn him. When he realized he was out of earshot,
he flew as quickly as he could to reach him, but Icarus was
too far away.

By the time Icarus opened his eyes, it was too late.
His wings were almost bare skeletons. He flapped and flapped
but the air just whistled through their empty frames and he
began to fall.

Daedalus could only watch, his eyes filling up with
helpless tears, as his son plummeted though the air, flapping
his useless, broken wings, and plunged into the deep,
blue sea. When Daedalus reached the spot where
Icarus had disappeared, all that was left was
a scattering of pale feathers floating
on the water.

Atalanta
and the golden apples

Deep in the forest, in the dead of night, a man put down a little bundle and walked away muttering to himself, "What use is a daughter anyway? Girls can't fight or look after themselves. They just eat you out of house and home until you eventually marry them off. Getting rid of her now will save me a lot of trouble." A pitiful wail pierced the night air behind him, but he pulled up the hood of his cloak and hurried away.

In the shadows, a mother bear pricked up its ears at the cry. It followed the noise until it came to a baby wrapped blankets, lying in the leaves. When the bear sniffed the baby, she stopped crying, and patted its nose with her tiny hands.

Gently, the bear took the blankets in its mouth, and carried the child home. It laid her between its two warm, furry cubs, and settled down to suckle them all.

After Atalanta was nursed by the bear, she was raised by hunters. It may be that they were all sent by Artemis, the goddess of hunting and wild animals, and protector of young children.

One morning twenty years later, the same forest rang out with hunting cries as a group of young men on horseback charged after a boar. "Whoever kills the beast can take it home," shouted Prince Meleager, letting an arrow fly and narrowly missing the boar's bristly back.

His companions jostled for the lead, their horses gleaming with sweat. Suddenly, another hunter appeared out of nowhere and overtook them on foot. For a moment, all they saw was a tumble of long, black hair as the skin-clad figure sprinted ahead of their horses. The hunter took aim and let an arrow fly.

There was a squeal from the boar as the arrow met its mark, and the men galloped up to find the newcomer standing over the dead animal, smiling broadly. To their astonishment, the hunter was in fact a huntress, and an extremely beautiful one at that.

"Who are you?" asked Meleager when he'd managed to find his tongue.

"My name's Atalanta," replied the young woman.

"Well Atalanta, you've won. The beast is yours to keep," Meleager said.

Atalanta slung the boar's body over her shoulder.

"Wait a minute," one of the other men protested. "You may have lost your head over her, Meleager, but you're not giving her our kill. She's a girl."

Atalanta narrowed her eyes. "This girl killed the boar before any of you," she said coldly. "And if you try to steal it from her, you'll be sorry." She turned on her heels and disappeared back into the forest.

Atalanta's reputation spread, and soon everyone
was talking about her bravery and beauty. Countless men
asked her to marry them, but Atalanta scorned them all.
Eventually, she tired so much of being asked that she sent
her latest suitor home with an announcement. "She says
she'll only marry a man who can outrun her in a race,"
he laughed to his friends. "I'm racing her next week."

"What happens if you lose?" asked one of the friends.

He snorted. "I die by her hand, apparently. But I'll
hardly lose against a woman."

The race attracted a large number of spectators,
and Atalanta turned up at the allotted time, with her bow
and arrows slung over her shoulder. She joined her suitor
on the starting line. "You'll never keep up with me carrying
those," he smirked. "You'd better put your weapons down."

Atalanta shook her head. "I don't need to," she said.

They crouched at the start, and somebody shouted,
"Ready? Set? Go!"

Atalanta's suitor sprinted away, entirely confident
of his success, but Atalanta streaked ahead, leaving him for
dust. She reached the finish in no time at all, to incredulous
cheers from the crowd.

But then she turned, drew an arrow and fired. The
arrow shot her suitor right through the heart. The crowd fell
silent with shock, and Atalanta turned to them and asked,
"Does anyone else want to try?"

All was quiet and then, to everyone's astonishment,
a man pushed forward through the crowd. "I'll race you,"
he said. "No woman can beat me."

Atalanta sighed. She gestured to the starting line, and they both took their places. Once more, the starter shouted, "Go!" and both figures set off at a sprint. But even though the second suitor put all his effort into the race, he fared no better. Atalanta ran like a deer, and by the time she crossed the finish, her competitor was only halfway down the course.

Coolly, she drew another arrow, aimed and fired. The suitor dropped dead not far from the man before him.

Atalanta glared fiercely at the spectators. "Anyone else?" she demanded. But nobody dared even meet her eye, and so she stalked away, leaving them to bury their dead.

Word of the challenge she had set spread across Greece, and more men journeyed from miles around to win her hand in marriage. By this time, they all knew the dangers. But, lured by Atalanta's beauty, they raced her nonetheless. One after another, each of them lost and she killed them without a second thought.

A handsome young man named Melanion came to watch every single race. He thought Atalanta was the most wonderful person he'd ever seen. She was heartless and wild, strong and independent, and he absolutely adored her. "There's no way I could beat her in a race," he thought despairingly, as he watched her long legs flashing past in a blur. "I'd be a lucky man to win her hand, but I need help."

He went to the temple of Aphrodite, the goddess of love, and knelt in front of her statue. "Noble goddess," he prayed. "Please help me. I've lost my heart to a woman I could never win on my own."

Many of the Ancient Greeks worshipped Aphrodite. They built numerous temples, shrines and statues to her, where they prayed or made offerings to the goddess in the hope that she might help them in love.

The air around him grew warm and he looked up to find the goddess standing over him. Her hair was shining and golden and her lips rosy and inviting. Most men found her irresistible but Melanion barely even noticed her beauty. All he could think of were Atalanta's fierce eyes and tumble of night-black hair.

Aphrodite knew this and it made her smile. "I will help you," she said. In her arms she held three shining golden apples, which she bent down and gave to Melanion. "During the race, drop one apple at a time in Atalanta's path," the goddess told him. "She won't be able to resist stopping to pick them up, and it will slow her down. Good luck," she added.

Melanion got to his feet a little shakily, clutching the apples. He certainly hadn't expected that. "Th–thank you," he stammered. But the goddess had vanished.

The next race day, Melanion arrived at the start line with the three golden apples tucked into a pouch at his waist. Atalanta strode up to him. "Are you next?" she asked.

"Call me a fool," answered Melanion, "but yes."

Atalanta frowned. "If you yourself think you're a fool, then why compete? I don't want to have to kill you. And you certainly won't be faster than me."

"Probably not," Melanion agreed. "Besides, I don't think anyone really deserves to win your hand. But I'd be giving up the greatest chance of my life if I didn't try. I think you're amazing."

Atalanta blushed, and then scowled and looked away in confusion. "Well, let's get on with it," she said hesitantly.

As they crouched at the starting line, Melanion took hold of one of the golden apples in his pouch. "Go!" came the shout, and Melanion broke into a sprint. Atalanta started running too, but a shining golden apple crossed her path and rolled away towards the crowd. She ran after it to pick it up, allowing Melanion to gain precious ground.

"It's working," he thought excitedly, glancing back over his shoulder. Atalanta waved the apple at him and then, to his dismay, began to catch up with him rather easily. "You dropped this," she said, holding the apple out.

Hurriedly, Melanion let the second golden apple fall. "You careless thing," Atalanta scolded, and fell back again to pick it up. Melanion ran for all he was worth, but she caught up without any trouble at all.

"You keep dropping these lovely golden apples," she said, running alongside him. "Someone's going to steal them if you're not careful."

Melanion was too out of breath to answer. Staring fixedly at the finish line, he did his best to speed up. He let the third apple fall in front of Atalanta, and saw her look at him questioningly before turning back to pick it up.

Melanion stumbled on, his chest burning as though it was on fire. Atalanta jogged along behind him with the three precious apples in her arms, only speeding up when her suitor crossed the finish line. The crowd let out a cheer, and Atalanta ran up to Melanion and grinned. "You lost these," she said, bundling the golden apples into his arms.

"But I won the race," Melanion panted.

"You've won more than that," Atalanta told him.

Melanion looked at her searchingly. "I don't want to win your heart in a race," he said. "But if you gave it to me freely I'd be the luckiest man that ever lived."

Atalanta laughed. "Then you should count yourself extremely lucky," she said.

From that moment on, the couple only had eyes for each other. They wandered away from the crowd, talking intently. Atalanta told Melanion all about her childhood in the forest, and Melanion told her all about how he'd watched every race she'd run, and had wondered how he could ever make her notice him. Without paying attention to where they were going, they arrived at Aphrodite's temple, wandered inside and sat down, hand in hand.

"I would have noticed you anyway," Atalanta said, confident of her new love, "but who gave you the clever idea of the golden apples?"

"Nobody," Melanion lied. "I thought of it by myself."

Atalanta kissed him. Then she glanced up at Aphrodite's statue. "Whoever needs the goddess of love, when you can find love all by ourselves, as we did?" she said.

"Yes who needs her?" Melanion laughed.

There was a sudden burning in the air. "You should give thanks where it's due, ungrateful Melanion," said an angry voice. The couple swung around to find Aphrodite behind them. She looked rather different from the way she had done the first time Melanion had seen her. Her lips were pressed together with anger and her eyes flashed dangerously.

146

"As for you," she turned on Atalanta, "you never would have noticed him in a million years if I hadn't given him the golden apples. You have found love, and I won't deny you that, but you've both behaved like beasts. So that's how you'll live from now on."

Atalanta and Melanion looked at one another in alarm, and each watched the other change before their eyes. Their skin sprouted golden fur; their hands turned into paws and their noses became furry muzzles. Sprouting whiskers and tails, they fell onto all fours and roared in dismay.

Aphrodite had turned them into lions.

The two beasts looked at one another helplessly. Nothing remained of the beautiful, athletic girl or the handsome man, but their eyes shone with love for one another just the same. Aphrodite watched as the pair of lions turned and walked away together into the deep, wild forest.

The Midas touch

"Good evening," King Midas said, peering out at the shadowy figure on the doorstep. The stranger stepped into the light, revealing a pair of pointed ears poking from a mop of silvery hair. He had a shaggy beard and a donkey's tail. Midas recognized him at once as a satyr.

"Allow me to introduce myself," the satyr said, "My name is Silenus. I'm a friend of Dionysus, the god of wine. He and I and a large party of others were passing through this area. I wandered off from the others and rather foolishly lost my way."

Midas's eyes had widened at the mention of Dionysus. Any friend of a god was not to be sniffed at. "Make yourself at home," he urged, showing in his guest.

The satyr sank gratefully onto a chair by the fire. "We were going to set up camp somewhere near here," he said, "in a grove of olive trees near the river."

149

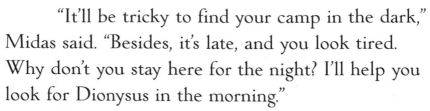

"It'll be tricky to find your camp in the dark," Midas said. "Besides, it's late, and you look tired. Why don't you stay here for the night? I'll help you look for Dionysus in the morning."

The next day, Midas showed Silenus the way to a nearby grove of olive trees. Sure enough, they found Dionysus and a huge party of followers camped there.

Dionysus himself came out to greet them. Midas gazed in awe at the god. He was a head taller than anyone else. His handsome face was framed with dark, lustrous curls and he had vines of jewel-like grapes dangling around his neck. "My dear friend," he cried jovially, throwing his arms around Silenus, "where have you been?"

"I got a bit lost," the satyr chuckled. "But King Midas here gave me a bed to sleep on for the night."

Dionysus clapped the king heartily on the back. "That's cause enough for celebration," he said. "Come, we'll have music and dancing and a feast to welcome an old friend and a new!"

Dionysus certainly wasn't a god to do things half-heartedly. At the click of his fingers, an entire roast ox appeared, complete with spit and fire. Servants hurried to carve the meat, and brought bowls of soft bread and sweet, musky grapes, not to mention barrel after barrel of berry-red wine. There were dancing girls and tumbling acrobats, pan-pipers and drummers; it was the best party Midas had ever been to.

After they had eaten their fill and were breathless with dancing, Dionysus came and sat next to King Midas.

Dionysus was the source of merriment and feasts wherever he went. His followers always liked a party. They consisted of satyrs...

maenads...

and nymphs.

150

"So, my friend," he said refilling the king's goblet, "how can I reward you for your kindness to Silenus? You can have anything you like!"

Midas's head spun with possibilities. "Anything at all?" he asked.

"Just name your wish," said Dionysus.

"Well in that case," Midas said. "I wish that from now on, everything I touch turns to gold!"

"So be it," said Dionysus.

Midas grinned from ear to ear. "I'll be the richest man alive!" he said.

Dionysus threw back his head and roared with laughter. Then, in the blink of an eye, the entire party vanished – Dionysus, the satyrs, the dancing girls and all the musicians were all gone. Midas found himself sitting alone on a moonlit hillside, his ears still ringing with the merry-making and music.

It was night already. How much time had passed? Had he really met a god? And had he been granted his wish? Midas got to his feet and hesitantly touched the nearest tree. Instantly the whole thing turned to gold, leaves and all.

Crowing with delight, he bent down and touched a flower. It too, turned to gold. "I'm rich, I'm rich!" Midas chortled, transforming leaves and pebbles and stuffing them into his pockets. He picked his way down the hillside and wandered home to his palace, touching a flower here and a dangling fruit there. By the time he got home, his path was littered with gold, all glittering in the light of the rising sun.

He pushed open the doors to his palace, laughing gleefully at their instant transformation. Hearing his master's voice, a servant came running.

"Bring me a feast," Midas ordered him, tossing the man a couple of gold pebbles. "Go right away. I want the finest food and wine gold can buy!" The servant hurried away, his eyes nearly popping out of his head.

Midas turned and looked at the rest of his palace. "Why settle for anything less?" he muttered greedily to himself, and he began to run his fingers across everything he could find – pottery bowls and vases of flowers, giant urns, tables and chairs, even the doors and floors and walls. He didn't stop until everything in sight had been turned to gold.

His wife came in rubbing her eyes, "Where have you been?" she asked sleepily.

"Consorting with gods," Midas boasted, "I've been blessed by Dionysus. I met him last night!"

"Where did all this come from?" his wife gasped as she looked around at all the gleaming gold.

"Me," said Midas proudly.

Just then the servant came in leading a line of others, carrying the finest feast gold could buy. Dish after dish was laid on the table.

"Sit down," Midas said to his wife, waving the servants away. "Let me tell you all about it."

His wife sank doubtfully into a chair. "We can't afford all this..." she began.

"Don't worry about that," Midas reassured her.

"We're rich beyond our wildest dreams." He picked up a dusky purple fig to put on her plate. Of course, the fruit turned to gold the instant he touched it.

"See?" he laughed, unperturbed. "I have this amazing new power!"

His wife stared at the fig, unable to believe her eyes. "But how?" she asked.

"It's simple," Midas said, "Like this..." he got up and whirled around the table like a magician, touching all the food and turning it all to gold.

"Have you taken leave of your senses?" asked his wife. "What good is gold food?"

"We can always buy more, darling." Midas answered. He strode over to his wife, and kissed her soft cheek. Immediately, her flesh cooled and hardened beneath his lips and his wife stopped stock still.

Midas stared in horror-filled fascination. Every strand of her hair, still tousled with sleep, was pure gold; her crumpled robe, her delicate throat, her slightly parted lips, her eyes, blank and gleaming. Every fingernail, every eyelash, was perfectly, terribly transformed.

He widened his gaze and took in the whole hall. Everything he'd touched was worth a fortune. He was surrounded by untold riches and yet the only thing that was truly precious to him had been lost.

"N—no," he choked miserably. He sank down into a chair, unthinkingly picked up a goblet of wine and dashed it down his throat. The wine became solid just as he swallowed. It slid lumpenly down his throat and settled heavily in his stomach. In horrified realization, he touched a piece of bread. Of course, it too instantly turned to gold. Only then did he fully understand what his wife had meant. "She's right," he murmured to himself. "Gold food is no good at all. I will die too. Oh, what have I done?"

When the servants returned to clear away the dishes, they found a feast all made of gold laid out on the table, and Midas with his head in his hands, weeping golden tears.

Suddenly he got up, ran out of the palace and back to the hillside where he had last seen Dionysus. He fell to his knees in despair. "Please undo my wish," he called to the empty air. "I beg you, noble Dionysus. Hear my plea."

"Now, now, don't upset yourself," said a jovial voice. He looked up to see Dionysus smiling down at him.

Midas threw himself at the god's feet. "Please can you take back the gift you gave me?" he begged.

Dionysus's smile grew a little cold. "I gave you exactly what you asked for."

"I was a fool to ask for it," Midas wailed. "'I've landed myself with a curse."

Dionysus shrugged. "Very well," he said. "It was meant as a reward, so I'll remove it. Go and wash yourself in the River Pactolus, and your touch will return to normal."

"And my wife — I turned her to gold by accident. Could you please turn her back as well?" Midas asked.

Dionysus frowned. "Gods aren't responsible for putting right all the foolish mistakes men make," he said impatiently, and promptly disappeared.

King Midas went to the river immediately and did as the god had told him. As he washed, streams of gold ran into the water. The river carried the flecks of gold along and, where it touched the banks, left them gleaming in the sand. Midas rubbed and rubbed at his body until the water ran clear. Then he waded to the riverbank and reached out hesitantly to touch a flower. To his relief, nothing happened.

He returned home with a heavy heart. Inside his palace, his poor gold wife was sitting motionless at the table, exactly as he'd left her. He stroked her gleaming cheek with his fingertips. "I'm sorry," he whispered. Then he called to his bewildered servants. "Get ready to leave this place," he ordered them. "I'm moving house."

That very day, Midas abandoned his palace and all his riches. He went into the forest and settled down to live in a simple wooden hut, far away from all the terrible reminders of his foolish, fatal mistake.

King Midas's secret

Since King Midas had gone to live in the forest, he'd become a fan of Pan's music. Pan was an impish goat-legged creature who wandered around the countryside, playing his wooden pipes wherever he went. His music could often be heard drifting through the forest. Midas spent hours trailing after the sound, humming along to the music, until eventually he knew the tunes off by heart. He'd never caught more than a glimpse of Pan, however, and he was longing to meet him.

One warm summer's afternoon, King Midas was strolling along by the side of a river, humming to Pan's lively playing nearby, when he suddenly spotted the musician himself, lolling under an oak tree. Pan saw him at the same time and stopped playing in surprise.

"Bravo! Bravo!" Midas cried, clapping his hands. Then he offered Pan his hand. "I'm King Midas," he said. "I'm a huge admirer of yours, so it's wonderful to meet you at last."

Pan grasped the king's hand and stood up.

157

"Thanks. Nice to meet you too," he said.

"I really love your music," Midas gushed. "It outstrips that of any of the gods. Apollo himself couldn't play a better tune than you."

Pan flashed him a mischievous grin. "I dare say you're right," he said.

At that moment, the air was filled with a strange quivering light, like sunlight reflecting off water. "Would you dare to repeat that to me in person?" said a voice behind Midas.

Midas swung around and came face to face with Apollo, the sun god. "Well I never," he said. Then, when he'd recovered himself a little, he added, "I'm sure your music is very good, Apollo, but Pan here plays some really fantastic tunes."

"That's right," said Pan mischievously, waving his pipes at the god. "I do."

A flush of indignation rose in Apollo's face. "Then you can prove it," he said. "In fact, we'll have a contest right here and now, to see whose music is better."

"What fun," said Pan.

"Tmolus, the mountain god, will be our judge," said Apollo. He turned to the purple mountain they could see through the trees and called, "Tmolus, wake up!"

The mountain shook the clouds of sleep from his eyes, and brushed trees from his ears. Birds flew away squawking, not having realized they'd been nesting in trees on the slopes of a sleeping god. "What do you want?" he rumbled at last.

When he heard the explanation, Tmolus agreed to be the judge. "But it had better be worth it," he warned.

Apollo nodded to his competitor. "After you," he said. So Pan raised his pipes to his lips and started to play. Music came bubbling and tumbling through the air. The rhythm was so catchy that no one within earshot could help but move in time. Midas leaped around, wiggling his hips and waving his arms. Rabbits hopped out of the undergrowth and bounced joyfully, while a line of birds began to waggle their tail feathers. Soon, even the mountain god was nodding his rocky head to the music. By the time Pan had finished, the entire forest was swaying.

"That was wonderful," boomed Tmolus. "Would you play at my daughter's wedding next month?"

"Sure," said Pan, grinning from ear to ear. "Beat that," he said to Apollo.

Solemnly, Apollo picked up his golden lyre. He began to stroke the strings gently with his fingers, and music rose from them like the sun rising in the sky at dawn. At first it was simple and beautiful, but it swelled up and up until it filled the air. Melodies wound around one another like vines. He played layer upon layer of music, faster, slower, gentler and louder, and all the layers combined into an unforgettable whole. It was stunning, immense and unending, like the very universe itself.

The effect on the listeners was extraordinary. The mountain god's eyes brimmed with tears, the forest creatures all crept closer, and the babbling river stopped flowing so that it could listen.

The lyre was a common Ancient Greek instrument a little like a small harp, which was strummed like a guitar.

159

When the last note died away,
the trees sighed in unison and the
river started quietly flowing again.
The mountain god shook his head.

"That was something else," he said. "I must admit,
Pan's music is great fun. Anyone who heard it would like it.
But you win hands down, Apollo. Your music is the best."

For a moment no one said anything. Even Pan was
still too moved by Apollo's music to speak.

Then Midas piped up. "I can't agree," he said.
"Apollo's music's fabulous, and all that, but it's a bit much
for me. What's wrong with a good old catchy tune? You
have to admit, no one gets people dancing like Pan."

Apollo turned on him, aflame with fury. "Those ears of
yours obviously aren't working properly," he said, pointing at
Midas. "Perhaps you'd hear better if I made them bigger."

160

A dazzling flash of light burst from his finger
and Midas felt a burning sensation around his ears.
"Ouch," he whined, clapping his hands to the sides of his
head. Something very strange was happening. His ears
didn't feel normal at all. They felt big and bristly and they
were *growing*. He stared at Apollo in alarm as they shot up
between his fingers. Pan burst into peals of laughter.

Midas rushed to the river's edge and looked down
at his reflection in horror. He had donkey's ears.

"Nobody will ever take me seriously again," he wailed.

"No change there then," Apollo muttered.

"They're not so bad," Pan giggled. "You could tie bows
on them or something."

King Midas stormed off into the forest. He waited until it was dark before going home, and then slipped into his palace unseen. He so dreaded anybody finding out about his ears, that he took to wearing a cap to hide them.

However, there was one person he had to tell – his barber. He couldn't very well get his hair cut with his hat on. The next time his barber came, he told the man his secret. "If you ever tell a single soul, I'll have your head chopped off," he warned.

Sometimes it's a terrible burden to be the keeper of a secret. The poor barber was bursting to tell someone – anyone – about King Midas's ears. It was too funny and too awful to be kept to himself.

Over the next few weeks, he could think of nothing else. His mind was so full of the secret that he almost let it slip on several occasions. When his wife asked, "What shall we have for dinner?" he blurted out, "Ears!" and then had to correct himself. "I mean – erm – some ears of corn..." When his assistant asked, "How many appointments do we have today?" He absent-mindedly replied, "Ears," and then had to cover his mistake: "I mean a year's worth of work!"

It was no good. If he didn't tell, he was going to let this secret slip at some point anyway and end up paying for it with his head.

That evening, he went out for a stroll before bedtime. "I'm just going to get a breath of fresh air," he told his wife. "Clear my ears – er – mind. You know."

She gave him a very strange look and he set off hurriedly. He wandered through fields near his house

until he came to the river. There wasn't
a soul to be seen in any direction. So there,
on the riverbank, among the reeds, the barber
dug a little hole. He bent low to the ground and
put his lips to the hole. "King Midas has donkey's ears,"
he whispered, and quickly filled in the hole with soil.

"I've said it," he sighed, relieved, and he went home
to his wife and slept more soundly than he had in weeks.

Down on the riverbank, in the dead of night, the
reeds near the hole rustled in the breeze, softly repeating
the barber's words. The whisper passed from reed to reed,
spreading all along the riverbank.

In the morning, a farmer came in from the fields
chuckling. "Guess what I heard the reeds whisper?" he said
to his wife. "King Midas has donkey's ears."

His wife told her friends when she went to market,
and her friends told their children, and the children told
their teachers who told their families, and very soon the
whole town was laughing about it. "You'll never guess what
the people are saying about you," one of Midas's advisors
told him one morning. "That you have donkey's ears!" But
the laughter died in the man's throat as Midas turned
beetroot red and he realized that it must be true.

"Get my barber at once!" roared Midas. The poor
man was brought, quaking, in front of the king, and lost
his head that very day. But despite the severity of the
punishment, King Midas remained a laughing stock for the
rest of his life. And if you listen carefully to the reeds on a
river bank, you might hear them whispering about it still.

163

Orpheus's journey into the Underworld

Orpheus was the greatest musician on earth. His music had an unbelievable effect on all who heard it. Whenever he played his lyre and sang, timid wild creatures would creep out of their hiding places to listen, trees would bend closer to him and winds would stop whistling. As a young man, he had been employed on ships to calm dangerous seas with his soothing music.

With such talents, Orpheus was never short of admirers, but his heart belonged to one girl alone – gentle Eurydice. He loved her so deeply that when he sang of his feelings, trees sprang into blossom overhead and the sunbeams danced for joy.

Eurydice loved Orpheus every bit as much. So, when he asked her to marry him, she nearly burst with happiness. But the very day after their wedding, disaster struck.

They were walking hand in hand through the forest when suddenly Eurydice cried out in pain. She collapsed into Orpheus's arms, her face deathly pale and her breath coming in short gasps.

"What happened?" he asked urgently. She pointed to her ankle, where Orpheus saw two tiny red toothmarks. She had been bitten by a poisonous snake. Moments later, Eurydice was dead.

Orpheus was inconsolable. "Why did it have to happen to her?" he wept. "Why now? We'd barely begun our life together."

Long after her funeral, he sat by her grave, hollow-eyed and ashen-cheeked, unable to accept that she was gone. Friends tried their best to comfort him, but there was little they could say. Eurydice's death made no sense to anyone.

Once, Orpheus saved an entire ship's crew from being lured to their deaths by creatures called sirens. The sirens began to sing their famously irresistible song to make the crew steer the ship onto the rocks. But Orpheus simply played a better song, and drowned them out.

Day after day, Orpheus sat motionless by his wife's grave. The summer faded. Trees shed their leaves like tears around him, and the sun's warmth ebbed away.

Then one day, quite suddenly, Orpheus got to his feet and began to walk. He walked all day and all night, and all through the next week until he came to a deep, dank cave with a still pool of water inside. In the pool lived a pretty water nymph, who swam over when she saw him.

"Hello, Orpheus. Won't you sing me a song?" she asked sweetly, for she had met him once before, and recognized him by the lyre he still had clutched under his arm.

166

So Orpheus played. He sang to the nymph about his desolate sorrow at his wife's sudden death. "I need to journey into the Underworld to bring her back," he sang.

The nymph's eyes brimmed with tears and she pointed wordlessly to a small opening in the back of the cave.

Orpheus nodded his thanks and set off into the dark tunnel. Down and down it wound, past roots of trees and seams of gleaming metal in the rock, deeper and deeper he descended below the earth. The darkness became so intense that soon Orpheus couldn't even see his hand before his face, but still he strode on fearlessly.

Gradually, a strange, pale light filtered onto his path, and the tunnel widened into a cavern full of enormous stalactites that dripped onto the stone floor, echoing eerily. Through the cavern ran an underground river, at the bank of which a dark, haggard figure stood hunched in a boat. It was the ferryman, Charon, whose job it was to ferry the dead over to the Underworld.

All around, shadowy souls of dead people were drifting down to the river. Some were old and some were young, some had terrible battle wounds, missing limbs or eyes, whereas others bore no signs of how they had died. They all crowded to the bank, weeping and moaning and clutching coins to pay the ferryman for their passage to the Underworld.

Orpheus joined them, shivering as their cold shadow-bodies brushed against his warm, living flesh. When he reached the boat, Charon looked at him sharply.

"I don't know what you're doing here," he said. "I only take the dead across."

"My wife died not long ago," Orpheus said. "I've come to take her home."

Charon stared at him in disbelief. "It's a one-way journey into the Underworld," he said. "You can't take people back to the world of the living. It's impossible."

Orpheus simply replied, "I have to. I can't live without her."

"People lose loved ones all the time," Charon answered unsympathetically. "It's the way of things. Do you suppose these people here don't have loved ones they left behind? You should consider yourself lucky. At least you're still alive."

There was a murmur of agreement among the dead, and they began to jostle past Charon, handing over their coins as they went to get onto the ferry.

"You don't understand," Orpheus said very quietly. And he raised his lyre and began to sing. He sang of his love for Eurydice, and how gentle and sweet she was. He sang of how she had died in his arms so suddenly the day after their wedding.

The shadowy dead turned and watched him as he sang. The music was so heartrendingly sad that their eyes filled with tears, and they fell back to allow him onto the ferry boat in front of them.

Even Charon, whose heart was as hard and cold as marble, rubbed his hand over his eyes and gruffly said, "Get in."

A living body weighs more than a dozen dead souls, so Charon had to take Orpheus across the river alone. He paddled silently across the dull water eyeing Orpheus, who clutched his lyre and said nothing.

On the far bank was a pair of enormous gates, wrought from darkly gleaming metal. The moment Orpheus stepped off the ferry, a monstrous three-headed dog leaped out of the shadows, snarling and slavering ferociously. It bared its three sets of teeth and lunged towards him, ready to eat him alive. Orpheus leaped back hurriedly, and raised his lyre.

He sang to the beast of his love for Eurydice, and how gentle and sweet she was. He sang of how she had died in his arms so suddenly the day after their wedding and of how his life had no meaning without her. He sang on sorrowfully until tears spilled from the dog's six bloodshot eyes, and it lay down at his feet and whimpered with sympathy.

Stepping past the monster, Orpheus pushed open the gates and entered the palace of Hades, god of the Underworld. Inside, polished black floors reflected twisted pillars leading up to a dark, vaulted ceiling that echoed with the distant wails of wandering souls.

Orpheus hurried through the palace until he found King Hades and Queen Persephone sitting on thrones. They were surrounded by crowds of shadowy dead, all waiting to find out which part of the Underworld they were destined for — the dark pits of Tartarus, or the garden paradise of the Elysian Fields.

All the dead surged forward when they saw
Orpheus, and touched his warm body with their
cold shadow fingers. "He's alive," they whispered
in wonder. "Remember what that felt like?"
Orpheus shuddered but did not shrink away.

"Leave him," commanded Hades, and the shadows
fell back. "What makes you so bold as to come here
before your time?" the king demanded.

"I've come to collect my wife," Orpheus said.
"I've come to take Eurydice home."

Persephone barked a cold laugh. "What makes
you think you can have her back?" she asked.

"I cannot live without her," said Orpheus.
"It must have been some dreadful mistake."

Persephone and Hades shook their heads.

"It was no mistake," Hades said firmly. So again,
Orpheus got out his lyre and began to sing.

He sang of his love for Eurydice, and how gentle and sweet she was. He sang of how she had died in his arms the day after their wedding and how his life had no meaning without her. He sang of how he would rather wait in the Underworld until he died than leave without her. He sang and sang, and his song drifted through the palace and out into the land of the dead. He sang until every single soul in the Underworld was sobbing and wailing for an exception to be made.

Orpheus kept on singing until Persephone turned to her husband and said, "We have to give this man his wife back." And he continued to sing until Hades nodded in agreement. Then he fell to his knees in gratitude.

Eurydice herself had heard the song, and was already waiting outside the palace when the guards went to fetch her. As soon as she was called, she hurried into the room. Orpheus tried to hug her, but his arms went straight through her shadowy body. Instead, he stared into her eyes, drinking her up in his gaze.

Then Hades spoke up. "Usually you cannot undo what has been done, whether it be a deed or a death. We are making a single exception to this rule. But there are two conditions. As you return to the land of the living, Orpheus, you must lead the way and your wife will follow. Until you both reach the light of the sun, neither of you may speak to one another, and you may not look behind you, Orpheus. If you so much as glance back, your wife will remain here forever. And you will not be permitted to come here again until you die."

Orpheus nodded. "I understand," he said. "Are you ready?" he asked Eurydice.

She nodded.

After one long last look at her, he turned and led the way out of the palace. As he walked passed the gates and the monstrous guard dog, Charon was just pulling up to the riverbank with a ferryload of dead souls. Some of them nodded to Orpheus, and one whispered, "You did it. Good for you."

Orpheus smiled nervously and got into the ferry boat. Not turning to look at Eurydice was harder than he'd thought. He stared hard at the far bank as he waited for his wife to climb aboard. Eurydice was so light the boat didn't rock or move in the least. In fact, Orpheus couldn't even tell that she was there, aside from Charon's brief nod to him before they set off.

When they reached the other side, Orpheus thanked Charon for his help and got out of the boat. He waited on the bank for a moment for Eurydice to get out of the boat behind him. Then he set off on the path leading upwards. He walked quickly and quietly, his body longing to reach the light and get it over with, and his ears straining for any movement to reassure him that his wife was behind.

There was none. Eurydice's footsteps were so light they made no sound whatsoever, and all he could hear was the dripping of the stalactites, his own footfall, and the rustle of his cloak. Orpheus drove himself onwards, staring fixedly ahead. "Whatever you do," he told himself silently, "don't look back."

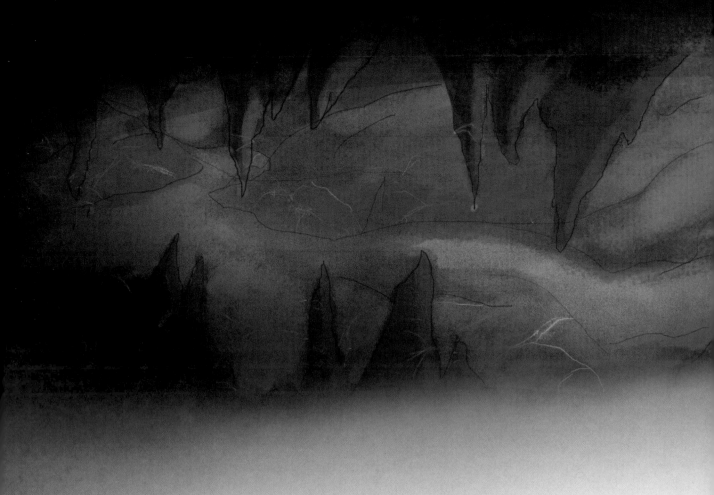

The path seemed to go on forever,
and all the way they walked in silence, through
the silent weight of the damp underground, past seams
of metal in the rock, up and up to the land of the living.
As the path wound through tangles of tree roots, at last
Orpheus caught sight of a small circle of bright daylight,
shining like a jewel ahead of him. They were almost there.

As he hurried closer to the light, he could almost feel
the warmth of the sun on his skin. "We've nearly made it,"
he cried. But in his excitement and relief, he forgot himself.

In a moment he would regret for the rest of his life,
Orpheus turned around.

Eurydice was right behind him, so close he could
see the horror in her eyes. But as soon as he turned,
she began to slip back the way they had come.

She reached out her hands to him
but some invisible force was pulling her back.

She was swept away, until the darkness swallowed her
up entirely. The last thing Orpheus saw of his wife was her
pale, beloved face.

Numb with grief, Orpheus turned and walked the
last few steps into the warmth of the sunlight. Without
even realizing what he was doing, he raised his lyre and
began to sing.

He sang of his love for Eurydice, and how gentle and
sweet she was. He sang of how she had died in his arms the
day after their wedding and how, against all odds, he had
journeyed into the Underworld to get her back. He sang
of how he had turned at the last moment and lost her all
over again. He sang and sang until the sky itself wept with
sadness and the whole world mourned with him.

But it made no difference. Eurydice was gone for
good this time, and there was nothing anyone could do to
bring her back.

Bellerophon
and the
flying horse

Welcome Bellerophon," the king smiled at the fresh-faced young man striding up to his throne. "It's wonderful to have you to stay."

"Your son-in-law asked me to give you this," Bellerophon told him, and handed the king a letter.

That night the king held a feast to welcome his guest, and they spent many days together talking, going riding and generally getting to know one another. They had such a pleasant time that the king forgot all about the letter.

On the tenth morning of the young man's visit, he found it again, and broke the seal. As he read, his blood ran cold. "Bellerophon must die," the message said. "He offended my wife – your daughter – terribly while he was staying with us, and no good can come of him staying alive. I trust you will see to it."

The king was very troubled by this letter. He'd seen nothing in Bellerophon's manner over the last few days that would suggest he was anything other than a likeable, lively young man. Besides, he had welcomed him into his home — he couldn't very well kill a guest. On the other hand, if this young man had indeed done something so awful his son-in-law wanted him killed, he couldn't very well do nothing.

"Is something bothering you?" Bellerophon asked him at lunch. "If there's any way I can help, just ask."

The king looked at the young man thoughtfully and suddenly he had an idea. "I was wondering," he said, "whether you would be brave enough to go on a quest."

No young man likes to admit he is anything other than brave, and Bellerophon was no different. "Of course," he said boldly.

"There is a terrible monster in my kingdom known as the chimera," said the king. "Have you heard of it?"

The sudden pallor of Bellerophon's cheeks answered the question well enough.

"It needs killing," the king went on, feeling rather sorry for his guest. "Only the strongest, bravest of men could attempt such a thing. What do you say?"

"I'll certainly try," Bellerophon answered, with only the tiniest tremor in his voice.

Later on, when Bellerophon had gone to bed, the king scribbled a note to his son-in-law saying, "I have sent the boy on a quest that he can hardly hope to survive. I hope that is enough for you."

That night, Bellerophon tossed and turned in his

bed. "How am I to slay the chimera?" he muttered to himself. "It's said to have the head of a ferocious lion that tears to pieces anyone who comes from the front, the head of a mighty serpent which attacks anyone who comes from behind, and the head of a fire-breathing goat between. How can I even get near enough to attack it? May the gods help me."

"You need to approach it by air, of course," said a strong, resonant voice. Bellerophon was extremely surprised to find a powerful-looking woman standing at his bedside. She looked remarkably like the statues of the goddess Athena he'd seen in temples.

He rubbed his eyes, thinking he must be asleep, but Athena was still there, looking down at him "The air?" he asked her in bewilderment. "I can't fly."

The goddess's lips curled upwards a little at the edges. "No," she agreed, "but there is a wild, winged horse called Pegasus that can." She handed Bellerophon a golden bridle. "Approach him quietly while he drinks from a pool. If you can catch him with this, he will be yours to ride. Attack the chimera from the air for the best chance of defeating it."

"But—" Bellerophon began.

The goddess reached forward and touched her fingertips to his eyelids. "Sleep now," she said, and he knew nothing more until morning.

Bellerophon awoke to find a golden bridle clutched in his hands. "It wasn't a dream," he whispered to himself. "If a goddess thinks I can do this, maybe I have a chance after all."

The chimera came from a monstrous family. Its siblings included Cerberus, the three-headed guard dog of the Underworld, and a swamp-dwelling serpent with many heads, known as the hydra.

Cerberus

Hydra

Over breakfast, he asked the king whether he knew of a wild, winged horse called Pegasus.

The king nodded. "Many have tried to catch him — it is impossible."

"If I can tame him, it may help me in my quest to kill the chimera. Can you tell me where to find him?" Bellerophon asked, and the king told him all he knew, hoping despite himself that the young man would succeed.

Carrying nothing but a spear and the golden bridle, Bellerophon walked until he reached the forest where Pegasus lived. In the middle of the forest was a quiet, shaded lake. It was a hot day, and the breeze across the cool water was welcome relief from the beating sun. "A wild horse might well come here to drink," he thought to himself, and he settled down to wait.

Before long he heard a soft flapping noise. He looked up to see a pearl-white horse flying gracefully through the air on feathered wings. It swooped down through the trees and landed by the lake where it looked around, sniffing the air for danger.

Bellerophon didn't move a muscle. He had chosen a hiding place downwind of the lake, so the horse wouldn't catch his scent. It seemed to work, for Pegasus lowered his head to the water and began to drink.

Bellerophon got to his feet and crept stealthily towards the winged horse. Only when he was very close did Pegasus finally see him. The horse reared and pummelled the air with his golden hooves, but Bellerophon darted beneath them and threw the bridle up over his nose.

It slid into place, and Pegasus tossed his head wildly trying to escape. Bellerophon clung to the reins and spoke to him in a low, soothing voice. Whether it was due to his voice or some magical effect of the bridle, he couldn't tell, but the horse calmed down surprisingly quickly.

Bellerophon stroked his neck gently for a few moments, and then climbed onto his back. At once, Pegasus leaped into the air and began to flap his pearl-white wings. He flew up between the branches and into the open sky. With the slightest tug of the reins, Pegasus turned and flew low over the treetops; another tug and they soared high into the clouds. It was the smoothest and most exhilarating ride of Bellerophon's life.

Very soon he felt confident enough to tackle the chimera. So he flew on Pegasus's back to the plains where the king had told him the monster lived. He scanned the barren, scrubby ground below until he saw something prowling around beneath, and swooped down lower to take a closer look. It was the chimera. The beast was every bit as strange and terrifying as the stories suggested, and even bigger than Bellerophon had expected.

He headed for the monster, urging Pegasus into a dive. Hearing the flapping wings, the chimera's giant serpent head hissed and looked up. Bellerophon thrust his spear at it but the serpent writhed aside and he missed. It wrapped itself around his spear, spitting venom. Pegasus struggled to gain height as the serpent pulled on the spear. But Bellephoron managed to wrench it free and they flew back up to safety.

Then they wheeled
around and plunged into a second
attack. This time, the chimera's lion head
bared its teeth and roared ferociously as Pegasus swooped past.
Bellerophon leaned right out and jabbed his spear into its neck.
The lion head roared in pain and the beast swung its great
claws at them. Pegasus pulled up just in time and they circled
above the monster. It was bleeding a little from the neck
wound, but it looked more fearsome than ever.

The goat head glared up at them with its sickening yellow eyes, as they swooped down a third time. As Bellerophon leaned forward to strike again with his spear, the goat head mouth opened and streams of flames shot into the air. Without flinching, Bellerophon thrust the spear through the flames, deep into the monstrous creature's throat.

As he pulled the weapon free, the tip broke off in the monster's throat. The chimera blew another furious blast of flame at them, but then suddenly it began to choke and gasp. The fire was so hot it had melted the metal spear tip inside its throat.

The chimera writhed as the molten metal entered its blood. The serpent, lion and goat heads all bellowed at once, and the deafening cries echoed across the plains, making animals tremble and scatter in terror. Pegasus shuddered and flew higher in an attempt to escape the unbearable noise, and Bellerophon clamped his hands over his ears in pain.

But all at once the chimera fell silent, and it slumped to the ground, dead.

Bellerophon could scarcely believe it. "We did it!" he cried, patting Pegasus's pearly neck. "I couldn't have done it without you."

The horse snorted proudly in answer. After circling the chimera's dead body one more time, they set off triumphantly for the king's palace.

When the king saw Bellerophon land in the courtyard on the winged horse, he rushed out to greet him.

At Lycia, where this story takes place, traces of the chimera still remain, as fire-breathing vents in the rocks that belch out flames from underground.

184

"You must have had the gods on your side to be able to tame this creature. My son-in-law will have to believe in your goodness now," he said. "Did you kill the chimera as I asked?"

"I did," Bellerophon replied. "But what do you mean about your son-in-law?"

The king sighed. "He sent me a note demanding that I kill you as you had deeply offended his wife, my daughter," he said. "I didn't want to kill you. So I sent you on this quest to prove yourself. But tell me, is it true what he said?"

Bellerophon flushed to the roots of his hair. "It is," he admitted. "But I didn't know what to do not to offend your daughter in the circumstances. It pains me to have to tell you, but she took a liking to me behind her husband's back. When I refused to kiss her, she said she'd have me thrown out in disgrace. So I made my excuses and left the next morning so as not to cause any more trouble. Please believe me."

"I do believe you," the king said. "Besides, not even my son-in-law will be able to deny your worth now you've killed the chimera. You have nothing more to worry about. Come inside, and let's celebrate."

While Bellerophon was welcomed happily back into the king's palace, Pegasus was led to the palace stables, where he was rubbed down and given oats and clean water to drink. The beautiful winged horse and his heroic new master became famous throughout the land, and they had many an adventure together in the years to come.

Eros
and
Psyche

Psyche was such a sweet girl, and so breathtakingly beautiful, that people went out of their way to do things for her. Strangers would offer to carry her bags, flower sellers would give her unexpected posies, and fruit sellers always saved the sweetest figs for her.

Her two elder sisters married rich kings from exotic lands, but to Psyche's dismay, nobody came to ask for her hand in marriage. The fact was that her beauty was so startling, men were afraid to ask. People utterly worshipped her, a fact that made Aphrodite, the goddess of love, absolutely livid.

"Who does that girl think she is?" the goddess raged to her son, Eros. "I don't care how pretty she is. No human can be worshipped like a goddess. Eros, I want you to bring her down a peg or two. Fire one of your love arrows into her heart, and make her fall in love with the ugliest person you can find."

"Your wish is my command," said Eros, and he flew off at once to carry out his mother's request.

When he came upon Psyche, she was chasing butterflies in a field near her house. Her hair was a mess and her cheeks were flushed with running. He'd been expecting to find someone proud and vain, but this was the most charming girl he'd ever seen. Right there on the spot, he fell head over heels in love with her himself.

"My mother will be furious if she finds out I'm in love with Psyche," he thought, "but I can't do as she asked."

Eros followed Psyche home. He made himself invisible, so she wouldn't notice him flying above her. His heart turned over as he heard her say to her parents, "Do you think anyone will ever want to marry me? I'm so lonely."

"Your turn will come," her father told her, stroking her hair. But after Psyche had gone to bed he sighed. "It doesn't make any sense that Psyche has no suitors," he said to his wife. "She's the sweetest girl alive. Maybe we should ask the gods to send us a sign."

Eros couldn't bear to miss his chance. "The gods will answer your prayers," he called solemnly. "Send Psyche alone to the top of the nearest mountain, and she will be taken to meet the husband of her dreams."

"Did you hear that?" whispered Psyche's mother.

"Yes. Do you think it's some kind of trick?" said her husband, peering out of the window.

"Do not doubt the word of the gods," said the voice, sounding rather stern this time. "Or you will spoil Psyche's good fortune forever."

The next morning, Psyche stood on the top of a mountain in the bright sunshine, feeling excited and more than a little nervous. She waved at her father and mother in the field far below.

Just then, she felt a mild breeze, and the West Wind swept her gently off her feet and carried her off the mountain top. It was an extraordinary feeling but Psyche wasn't afraid. She floated far, far away, until eventually the wind set her down in a meadow full of flowers.

At the side of the meadow was a forest, and in the middle of the forest stood a golden palace. Psyche walked up to the doors of the palace and they opened by themselves. "Is anyone home?" she called timidly as she stepped inside. There was no reply, but inside a table was laid with fresh fruit, cheese and bread that was still warm from the oven.

Psyche was hungry after all the excitement of the morning, and the palace seemed so welcoming that she sat down and helped herself to breakfast. After she had eaten her fill, she began to look around. There wasn't a single soul to be found, but everywhere she went, doors opened before her, and everything seemed to have been prepared just for her. The vases were filled with flowers she loved, and the countless rooms were all decorated exactly to her taste.

By evening, lamps around the palace had been mysteriously lit, and she found another table freshly laid with a delicious meal. After she had eaten, she was very sleepy. She discovered a lovely bedroom and felt so at home that, without a second thought, she slipped into the large, comfortable bed.

Born of the sun and the stars, there were four gods of the winds.

The West Wind brought light spring breezes.

The South Wind blew with the warmth of summer.

The East Wind sent the leaves falling from the trees at the end of the summer.

The North Wind was the chill of winter.

"I wonder if I will meet my husband tomorrow," she murmured to herself as she blew out the lamp. "I do hope I like him."

All the hairs on her body stood on end as a quiet voice replied. "I hope so too." She felt someone sit on the bed beside her. "Don't be afraid," the person said. There was such tenderness and warmth in the voice, that Psyche's fear slipped away immediately.

"I'm not," she said, rather surprised at herself. "Tell me, did you leave those wonderful meals for me?"

"Yes," said the voice. "I hope you enjoyed them — and that you like the palace?"

"Everything's perfect," said Psyche. "Thank you." She felt across the covers in the darkness, and found a warm hand. She and her mystery host talked shyly in the darkness, until eventually Psyche fell asleep.

When she awoke in the morning, the covers by her side were still warm but nobody was there. She got up to find breakfast laid out, and spent another day wandering alone around the palace, seeing no one but feeling as though her every need was taken care of.

That evening, she blew out her light and waited eagerly for her companion to return. They spent many happy hours together, chatting and getting to know one another. In the morning, she awoke again to find him gone.

A few weeks went by in the same way and, despite the strange nature of her new life, Psyche had never felt so happy. But she often thought about her family, and wondered if she would ever see them again.

One night she asked her companion, "Do you mind if I go home to visit my family? The last thing they saw was me being swept off the top of a mountain and I'd hate them to worry."

"You could send them a letter," suggested her companion. "The West Wind would take it for you."

"I'd really like to see them for myself," Psyche said. "Then they can see for themselves how happy I am. I'd hurry back to you. You needn't worry about that."

There was a moment's silence. Then her companion said, "I'm more worried they will think it strange that you never see me, and that they'll make you suspicious. Believe me, Psyche, it's for our own good. If you knew who I was, you'd be in great danger. I'd have to leave you right away."

"Nobody could make me suspicious of you," Psyche assured him. "I love you."

"I love you too," her companion answered warmly. "Very well. Go to the meadow tomorrow, and the West Wind will carry you home. After four days it will bring you back to me."

When Psyche went to the meadow in the morning, the West Wind scooped her up, carried her over the mountain tops and set her down outside her parents' house. Psyche's mother and father were overjoyed to see her. They couldn't hug her enough, and asked her all sorts of questions about her new life. When she told them she had never seen her beloved, they looked a little surprised, but her mother said, "Still, he must be a good man to make you so happy. I'm sure he has his reasons."

The next day, Psyche's two sisters came to visit, and were terribly curious about her husband-to-be. They weren't nearly as accepting when they learned she hadn't yet seen him. "If he's so good, why does he hide?" asked one.

"He must be an ugly monster!" said the other. "He's afraid you wouldn't love him if you ever saw him."

"That's it," squealed the eldest, rather pleased with the idea that her little sister's life wasn't so perfect after all.

Psyche shook her head. "I don't think he can be a monster," she said. "He's so good to me."

"Only because he can't believe his luck, you fool," her eldest sister scolded. "You'll end up with monstrous children if you carry on like this. Why don't you wait until he's asleep and then take a tiny peek?"

"He needn't know about it," added the other sister. "If you really love him, you can stay. But at least you'll know who you're living with."

Psyche didn't answer, but she couldn't forget her sisters' words. "I do love him," she thought. "But I suppose I have a right to know what he looks like."

After the four days were over, she said goodbye to her family, and stood outside the house again. Once more, the West Wind swept her up into the air, and took her back to the golden palace.

That night, she went to bed as soon as it was dark, and smiled in the darkness at the sound of his approaching footsteps. "I've missed you," he whispered.

"I missed you too," she replied. They hugged one another in the dark. He certainly didn't feel like a monster, but Psyche couldn't get her sisters' suggestion out of her mind. Her thoughts kept her wide awake until she heard her companion's breathing grow slow and relaxed. "He's asleep," she thought. "It won't harm if I just take a little look."

She crept out of bed, lit a lamp, and held it up over her sleeping husband. What she saw took her breath away.

Far from being a monster, he was more handsome than she could possibly have imagined. His hair and eyelashes shone golden in the lamplight, and his skin was glowing and soft. Suddenly she noticed a bow and arrows hanging from the head of the bed, and saw a pair of feathered wings spread out beneath him. Her companion was none other than Eros, the god of love himself.

Psyche gave a little gasp, and a drop of oil fell from her lamp onto Eros's chest. His eyes opened and he stared at her in horror. "What did I tell you?" he burst out angrily, getting out of bed and heading for the door.

"But what does it matter if I know who you are?" Psyche said. She followed him downstairs and out of the front door, where he took flight and left her standing there alone. "Oh what have I done?" she wept. "I should have trusted him. I'll have to find him and make amends."

As dawn broke over the horizon, she set off to look for him. Day after day, week after week, month after month, Psyche searched for her beloved Eros to no avail. He seemed to have vanished without a trace.

Then one day, she came to a temple with a statue of Aphrodite, the goddess of love, inside. She fell to her knees before it and prayed. "Please help me find Eros again. I love him so much and I'm sure he loves me."

"You stupid girl," said a scornful voice behind her. Psyche spun around to find Aphrodite standing there. "What makes you think my son could ever love you?"

"B—but you must know about it," stammered Psyche. "We lived together in a golden palace and he told me he loved me, but that I must never see his face."

Aphrodite turned crimson with fury. "So that's what he's been up to," she muttered. To Psyche she said, "I won't help you until you prove to me how much you love him. Outside is a mound of grains. I want you to go and separate them out into different sorts. Have it done by nightfall or you'll never see Eros again."

Psyche hurried outside, where she found a pile, as tall as herself, of wheat, barley and corn grains all mixed together. She began at once to pick out the tiny grains and put them into separate piles, but there were so many she didn't get very far before the light began to fade. Poor Psyche burst into tears. "I won't be able to do it in time, however hard I try," she sobbed.

A passing ant took pity on the beautiful girl. It brought back the rest of its colony, and together they set to work. By the time the sun had set, the ants had separated all the grain into three tidy piles. "I can't thank you enough," Psyche whispered to the tiny creatures as she dried her eyes.

When Aphrodite appeared a moment later, she didn't look at all pleased. "Well done," she said sourly. "Tomorrow I want you to collect a bundle of golden wool from the sheep that live on the hill over there."

In the morning, Psyche went straight to the hill to start her task. She didn't realize that the sheep weren't nearly as harmless as they looked. But the grass took pity on her and whispered to her on the breeze. "These sheep are dangerous. They'll kill anyone who goes near them. Wait until they are asleep, and then you can collect the wool from the bushes."

"Thank you for telling me," said Psyche. She retreated back down the hill until noon, when the sheep all settled in the shade and dozed off. Then she crept around the field, gathering all the wisps of wool that had caught on briar bushes, until she had as much as she could carry.

When she laid the golden bundle at Aphrodite's feet,

the goddess glowered at her, then turned white with anger. "Your next task is harder," she said coldly. "You must go into the Underworld and bring back a box of Persephone's everlasting beauty."

"B—but how can I possibly go into the world of the dead and ever come out alive?" asked Psyche, trembling with fear.

"Who said you could?" the goddess hissed nastily. "But I will make things very unpleasant for your beloved and your ugly self if you don't bring me that box. Now, go!"

Psyche wandered away sadly, and climbed to the top of the highest tower she could find. "There's no other way," she said to herself. "I'll have to die to get into the Underworld."

She was about to throw herself off the tower, when she heard a strange, echoing whisper on the wind. "You don't have to kill yourself. I can tell you another way to get into the Underworld." It was the tower itself that had taken pity on her. It told her exactly what she had to do to complete her next task safely.

With tears of gratitude in her eyes, Psyche thanked the tower and hurried away to complete the task.

Following the instructions the tower had given her, Psyche took two pieces of bread soaked in honey,

and two silver coins. Then she set off to find
one of the entrances to the Underworld.

She walked along the coast through deserted
scrubland, where no bird flew and no flower bloomed.
Eventually, she came to a sudden kink in the shoreline.
The tower had told her this concealed an entrance to the
Underworld. She peered past the tufted grass on the coast
and into the murky sea, but she couldn't see anything
unusual about it. So, taking a deep breath, she stepped
off the edge of the coast.

Instead of stepping into the sea as she would have
expected, she suddenly found herself in a long, dark tunnel.
Hearing the sound of a running water ahead, she walked
along until she came to an underground river.

Waiting on the bank of the river was a haggard
old man in a boat. "What are you doing here?" he asked
suspiciously. "Only the dead come to this place."

Psyche knew him very well to be Charon the
ferryman, whose job it was to take the souls of dead
people across the River Styx. "Aphrodite sent me to
see Persephone," she said politely. "I'd be grateful if you
could give me safe passage." She pressed a coin into the
ferryman's palm.

"Very well," he sniffed, tucking the coin into his robe.
He helped her onto the boat and pushed it slowly
across the river with a long pole.

On the far bank, Psyche
found an imposing pair of metal gates.
Guarding them was the most terrifying creature
she had ever seen. It was a monstrous three-headed
dog with a venomous-looking serpent for a tail.
The creature was Cerberus, the guard dog of the
Underworld. Its growl made her tremble as she
approached. But she tossed it a hunk of
honey-soaked bread, and hurried past
as the creature gobbled it up.

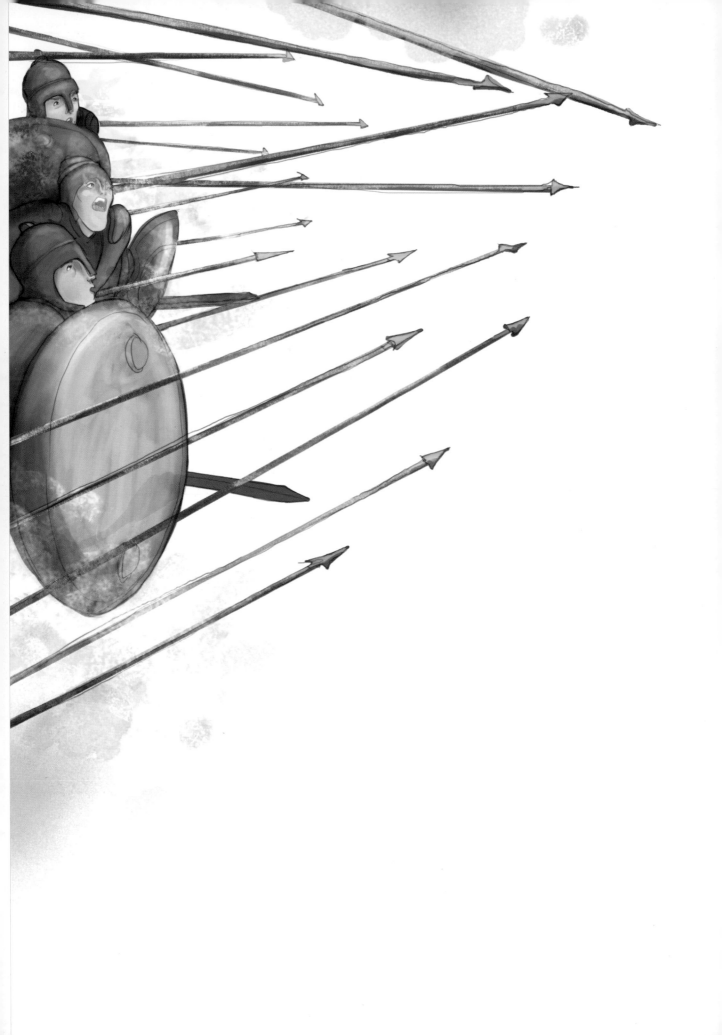

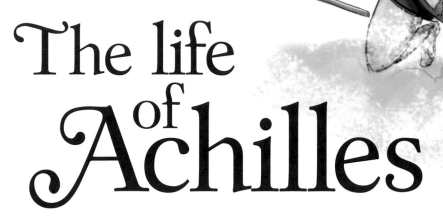

The life of Achilles

The moment Peleus spotted Thetis on the beach, he fell in love. Of course, he didn't know her name was Thetis, or that she was actually a sea goddess. All he saw was a beautiful woman walking out of the waves, with water dripping like diamonds from her long, red hair. He walked up to her, unsure of what to say. In the end, he blurted out, "I never believed in love at first sight before."

Thetis glanced at him scornfully. "You're only human," she said. "You don't know what you're saying." And she turned away.

"I don't know what you mean," Peleus protested. "I've never been so sure of anything in my life."

Thetis sighed. "It's easy for you to love me when I appear in this form," she explained, "but I'm a goddess. This is only one of my forms. I have many, many others, and there are times you'd think me a monster."

"I don't think so," said Peleus, taking her in his arms.

Thetis frowned, and the next moment, Peleus found himself struggling to hold on to an enormous shark with razor-sharp teeth. He gasped in shock, but he didn't let go.

At once, the shark changed and he found himself clinging on to a giant stingray, and then a fearsome sea serpent which wrapped itself around his body and squeezed the breath from him. Determined to prove himself, Peleus hung onto her. "I'm not letting go," he said obstinately, looking into the serpent's emerald eyes.

To his great relief, the serpent turned back into the lovely woman. "Perhaps you're different from most humans then," she said, and the look in her sea-green eyes made his skin tingle.

Not long after that day, the couple decided to get married. Thetis left her watery home for her husband's house on the coast. They were extremely happy together, and soon they had a child.

The baby was a boy, with a shock of red hair like his mother's, and a fiery cry to match. They named him Achilles, and Thetis held him close and murmured, "I'll make sure no harm ever comes to you, little one."

"We both will," Peleus said, putting his arms around the pair of them.

The next morning, Peleus awoke to an empty bed. He heard Achilles crying downstairs, so he hurried down the marble steps. He followed the cries to the doors of a little-used storeroom. "Thetis?" he called again. "Are you in there?"

The doors were locked, and with a rising
sense of panic, he burst through them into the
room. There he found Thetis, her face a mask of
concentration, holding their newborn baby by his
heels and dangling him into a blazing fire.

Peleus ran over and snatched Achilles from the
flames. "What do you think you're doing?" he shouted at
his wife. Miraculously, the baby was unharmed.

"I was making him safe!" Thetis replied indignantly.
Peleus stared at her in dumb astonishment.

"Any child of ours is half human and half god,"

205

Thetis explained. "If the human side is burned away in a magic fire, only the god side is left, which can't ever be harmed. But I hadn't finished, so now he's going to have weak heels forever…" Her voice trailed away when she saw the expression on her husband's face.

"You're trying to burn all of the human side – *my* side – out of our son?" he asked her in a low voice. When she nodded, he turned away with the baby in his arms and could not bring himself to look at her again.

That night, Peleus watched through the window as his wife padded down to the beach and slipped into the sea. He knew she wasn't coming back. He was heartbroken, but from that night, he turned all his attention to his son.

The years passed, and Achilles grew into a fearless boy. But despite his daring, the usual cuts and bruises of childhood were curiously absent. He never came to the slightest harm. When he reached the age of ten, his father decided it was time for him to have a proper education. "I'm going to arrange for old Cheiron to teach you," he told the boy.

"Who's that?" Achilles asked.

"He's a centaur – half man, half horse," explained Peleus. "He'll teach you how to hunt and ride, how to shoot an arrow and fight with a sword, and many other things that will make you a man, and me a very proud father."

Achilles's face lit up. He couldn't wait. The days dragged until the next week, when his father finally took him to the forest where he was to live with Cheiron throughout his schooling.

Cheiron was a wise, kind old centaur, who had taught lots of heroes, including Jason and Heracles, before Achilles.

Deep in the forest, the white-haired centaur galloped out of the trees to greet them. He embraced Achilles's father, and then grasped Achilles firmly by the hand and looked intently into his eyes. "Let's see what you're made of," he murmured, and Achilles shivered a little under the centaur's penetrating gaze.

After a moment, Cheiron said solemnly, "You will be glorious in war, my lad." Then he slapped Achilles on the back and laughed, "But first you have much to learn! Come along. The sooner you unpack, the sooner we can get started."

Cheiron's home was a network of caves set into a steep hillside. Inside, there was a grand hall with stone columns and an arched ceiling. Fresh spring water ran in channels, feeding several tumbling fountains, and a lush fern garden. Winding tunnels led to snug sleeping chambers that were lit through holes in the rocks above.

A dark-haired boy, only a little older than Achilles, appeared at the door of one of these chambers. "Hello. You must be Achilles," said the boy. "My name's Patroclus."

"What are you doing here?" Achilles asked.

"I'm Cheiron's pupil, just like you," Patroclus told him pleasantly. "We're going to have lessons together."

Their first lesson was a sparring match with wooden swords. Cheiron stood at the edge of a clearing, and called out directions as the two pupils fought one another.

Patroclus fought cautiously, defending himself solidly and waiting patiently for the right moments to attack. Achilles, on the other hand, launched himself recklessly

Patroclus had been a headstrong youth. Before he was sent to be trained by Cheiron, he had killed a boy after an argument over a game of dice.

207

into the fight. He scarcely defended himself at all, but moved as fast, and as unpredictably, as lightning. The boys fought to and fro, unable to defeat each other.

"Bravo," called Cheiron. "But Achilles, you keep leaving yourself exposed." As his two pupils continued to fight, he picked up a long thin branch. "In a true battle, another fighter could stab you here." He was about to poke Achilles in the ribs to illustrate his point, when Patroclus quickly turned and lopped the end off the branch.

"Unless of course," their tutor added, sounding amused, "you have a loyal friend to defend you." He lunged with his branch and flipped both boys' swords from their hands. "There ends our first lesson," he said.

The boys' education was everything they could have dreamed of. All day long they hunted and rode, shooting arrows and throwing spears until their aims were perfect. Gradually they became inseparable friends, not to mention strong, skilful warriors.

One day after a trip into town, Achilles came galloping back to the forest with news. "Queen Helen of Sparta has been kidnapped," he told his friend. "Some Trojan prince named Paris made off with her. Or rather, word has it she's run away with him for love. At any rate, her husband King Menelaus has declared war on Troy. He and his brother are gathering armies from all over Greece."

The friends rushed to Cheiron, and told him that they were going to sign up to fight. "It's our duty to go," said Patroclus.

"We can't miss the chance," Achilles added.

"Our names could go down in history!"

The centaur nodded as if he had been expecting the news. "It's time for you both to face your futures," he said. The boys said goodbye to their teacher that very day, and went home to spend one last night with their families before they sailed.

Achilles was sound asleep in his old bed when someone gently touched his face. He opened his eyes to see a woman bending over him. She had green eyes that mirrored his own, and water dripped like diamonds from her long, red hair. "Mother?" he whispered.

"Don't go to war," Thetis begged him. "I didn't have time to make you safe. You're vulnerable."

"What do you mean?" Achilles asked, sitting up.

His mother told him all about the magic fire, and the reason she had left when he was a baby. "So you have one weakness," she said finally, "your heels."

"But that doesn't have to stop me from going to war," Achilles said. "Other men don't have that kind of protection. Besides, nobody's likely to aim at my heels, are they?"

"Come away with me," Thetis persisted. "There's plenty of time for fighting yet."

Having only just met his mother, Achilles couldn't bear to disappoint her, and so he agreed. He followed her down to the beach, where a chariot made of seashells was waiting on the shore. They climbed into it and a pair of dolphins rose up from the waves, and began to pull them across the moonlit sea.

All night long, mother and son talked. Then at last, as the rosy-fingered dawn began to lighten the sky, they reached an island, where they went ashore.

"Put this on," Thetis said, handing Achilles a woman's robes. Very reluctantly, he did as she asked. "People will look for you," his mother explained. "And this way you will not be found."

"Who will look for me?" Achilles asked, but Thetis would not answer. She took him to a palace, and left him there in the care the king of the island.

The king was a friend of his mother's, and treated him very well. But Achilles hated hiding from the war, and itched to throw off his embarrassing disguise. So it was a relief to him when, very soon after, someone did indeed come looking for him. A fleet of ships arrived at the island, and the captain came ashore to see the king.

"I am Odysseus, King of Ithaca," the stranger announced. "I'm on my way to Troy, but I'm searching for a young man named Achilles. We've consulted the gods, who told us the Trojan War cannot be won without him."

"I don't know anyone by the name of Achilles," said the king.

Odysseus glanced around the room and his eyes lingered for a moment on Achilles's flushed face. He turned back to the king. "It seems strange that the hero of this war would be so cowardly as to try to avoid it," he said mildly. "Are you sure you don't know his whereabouts?"

Odysseus's journey was only just beginning. An oracle predicted that if he went to fight in the Trojan War, it would be many years before he could return home.

210

The king shook his head. But Achilles stood up and threw off his disguise. "Here I am," he said, hot with indignation. "Let me assure you, I'm no coward. When do we leave for Troy?"

They set sail the very next day, and soon their fleet joined the rest of the thousand ships all making for Troy. As Achilles stood on deck, a familiar figure appeared at his side. "Where have you been?" Patroclus asked, slapping him on the back. "I thought you were going to miss all the action!"

"Not for the all world," Achilles answered. Excitement rose in his chest as he and Patroclus gazed at the billowing sails spread out across the sea all the way to the horizon.

As they approached Troy, the beach glistened with the weapons of the waiting Trojan army. The Greeks raised their fists and gave a rousing battle cry as their boats neared the shore.

Even before they had drawn into land, Achilles leaped off the ship. He waded through the water and plunged straight into the battle without a second thought. Patroclus wasn't far behind.

Achilles fought like a tiger, leading the way through the enemy troops. Patroclus stayed close, following his friend's flame-red hair through the midst of a forest of flashing swords and bristling spears. Gradually, the Greek army drove the Trojans further and further up the beach, until they could do nothing but retreat behind the walls of their city.

The next day, the Trojans came
out to fight again. From dawn to dusk,
chariots charged and swords clashed; spears thrust
and men died. The Trojans stood firm, defending
their city; the Greeks fought fiercely, trying to
win back their queen. But neither side gave way.
As the evening drew near, the Trojans fell
back again behind their city walls, and
the Greeks returned to their tents
on the beach to bury their dead
and tend to their wounded.

After a week of fighting, Achilles was sitting by the boats one night, looking out to sea, when he saw a woman walk quietly out of the water. He went down to the shore to greet her. "Mother," he said, taking her hands in his. "I'm sorry. I couldn't carry on hiding from the war."

Thetis looked at him sadly. "If you went back home now, Achilles, you could live a long and happy life," she said.

"But if I stay," Achilles replied, "my name will be remembered by the world long after I'm dead."

His mother could only nod. She knew very well the fate that lay before him.

The war at Troy went on for many long years. Whenever it looked as if the Greeks were about to win, the Trojans would gain the upper hand. When the Trojans threatened to defeat the Greeks, the tide of battle would suddenly turn again. Neither side could overwhelm the other, and neither side would give up. It seemed as if the fighting would never end.

Then, one fateful day, a soldier came running to Achilles. "I have bad news," he told Achilles reluctantly, his eyes full of tears. "Patroclus is dead."

Everybody knew how close the two friends were — they had fought side by side on every single day of the war so far. But on this one day, Patroclus had gone off on his own. Achilles hadn't been there; he hadn't seen him fall; and he couldn't do a single thing to change it. Grief lit a flame of fury within him that some say frightened even the gods.

"Who killed him?" he asked through clenched teeth.

"The Trojan prince, Hector," answered the soldier.

Bent on revenge, Achilles stormed straight into the battle. He cut through swathes of Trojan soldiers, felling men like blades of grass as he tried to reach his friend's killer. But no matter which direction he approached, the prince was always well protected by his army.

Eventually, it was clear that Achilles wouldn't rest until he met Hector. So the Trojan prince sent a messenger to Achilles. He would meet him the next day in front of the city gates, where they would fight in single combat to the death.

As the sky paled into morning, Achilles drove his chariot up to the gates of Troy. As soon as he saw Hector there alone, he let out a fearsome battle cry and charged. Hector was a brave man, but his courage almost crumbled at the sight of this inflamed, god-like figure bearing down on him, white face glowering and red hair blazing.

At the last moment, Achilles reined in his horse and the two men locked eyes as the dust settled around them. By this time, Trojan warriors had lined the walls of their city, and the Greek troops had come up from the beaches to watch the two men fight. Every single one of them was silent, scarcely daring even to breathe.

Then Hector raised his spear. In a split second, Achilles had launched his own. It shot through the air so fast that Hector didn't stand a chance. The tip drove straight through his neck and killed him on the spot.

A triumphant roar went up from the Greek side.

But Achilles didn't cheer. He just stood and glared at his fallen enemy's body. Revenge hadn't lessened the pain of losing his friend one bit.

The grief he felt was so intense that suddenly something in him snapped. Stony-faced, he tied a rope around Hector's ankles, looping the other end onto the back of his chariot. Then he leaped onto the back of the chariot and set off. He drove all around the city walls, dragging Hector's body behind him.

Both the Trojans and the Greeks were horrified. This was no way to behave, even with the body of an enemy. But Achilles was beyond reason, and nobody dared stop him. He circled Troy again and again, dragging the body through the dust.

Eventually, Achilles returned to camp, with Hector's body still trailing behind his chariot. He threw down his weapons, his face like thunder, and went inside his tent. His comrades eyed one another nervously, but nobody dared speak to him.

Late that night, when everyone had gone to bed, Achilles had a visitor. He was sitting miserably on his bed with his head in his hands when a cloaked man slipped silently through the doorway. "Who are you?" Achilles demanded, springing to his feet.

The man drew back the hood of his cloak. It was Priam, the king of Troy. "I have come to claim my son's body," the elderly king said with great dignity.

Achilles shook his head angrily.

"I understand the pain of your loss, Achilles,

for I feel it myself," Priam said. He knelt at the young man's feet and looked up at him, tears glimmering in his eyes. "But you are able to bury your beloved friend," he said. "Please, let me bury my son."

Despite himself, tears sprang into Achilles' own eyes. Gently, he helped the king to his feet. "You must have the heart of a lion to come here alone like this," he said gruffly. "You can take him back."

He went outside and untied his enemy's body. The king took it home, and both sides agreed to stop fighting for eleven days out of respect for the dead.

After that, the battle resumed. Both sides were weary and disheartened by their losses. Only Achilles's fire seemed undiminished. He alone fought more and more brilliantly with each passing day. Some even believed that he'd win the war all by himself.

One day, he managed almost singlehandedly to drive a whole troop of Trojan soldiers into a frantic retreat. They rushed back into the city, and Achilles followed them through the city gates before the gatekeepers could shut them.

It was a rash move. He was surrounded by Trojans, the only Greek inside the city. But Achilles was fearless, and stood his ground without flinching. Amazingly, the Trojans began to back away from him. Then from their midst, a young man stepped forward. That man was Paris.

Prince Paris was young, like Achilles. He wasn't a natural soldier, but the whole war had started on his account, when he ran away with Helen, a Greek king's wife.

Helen became famous as Helen of Troy, and tales of her beauty spread all around the world. Because a war was fought over her, she is often known as the face that launched a thousand ships.

He had seen his brother Hector and countless soldiers go to their deaths as a result, and was determined to play his part in bringing the war to an end. He raised his bow and arrow and took aim.

"Is this the little prince who stole Helen of Sparta?" Achilles asked mockingly.

"She's Helen of Troy now," Paris replied, and he let his arrow fly.

His face fell as the arrow swooped low, and Achilles let out a scornful laugh and began to turn away. But whether the arrow was guided by luck or poor aim or, as some believed, the invisible hand of the gods, Paris couldn't have aimed his shot more wisely.

Just as Achilles turned away, the arrow hit him in the only vulnerable place on his body — the back of his heel. His whole body arched in pain, and he fell to his knees. The entire Trojan army, including Paris, watched in disbelief as the famous Achilles gasped his last breath, and sank to the ground, dead.

Nobody could believe their eyes. After all he had been through, the most invincible warrior they had ever known had finally been slain by a single arrow in the back of his heel.

But, Achilles was right. His name was remembered long after his bones crumbled to dust. He went down in history as the most glorious warrior ever to have lived. After his death, the war limped on for a few more years. It took a wily plan to draw it, finally, to a close.

But that's another story...

The giant wooden horse

"We're not going to win this war by brute force alone," Odysseus said to the weary Greek soldiers gathered around the camp fire after another day's fighting. "We have been at war for ten long years, and have lost so many good men. Some of our strongest warriors have fallen."

The men eyed Odysseus in the flickering firelight. "What are you saying we should do, Captain?" asked Menelaus, the king of Sparta. "Go home?"

Odysseus shook his head. "Not before we've beaten the Trojans," he said. "I'm suggesting we try a little brain power. Let me explain..."

Under the stars on the beach where the Greek army had their camp, Odysseus revealed his elaborate plan. He paced back and forth energetically as he talked, drawing shapes in the air and diagrams in the sand. Finally the men began to smile and nod. It was a very strange plan, not to mention a risky one, but they all agreed it might just work.

All through the night the weary men toiled, cutting down trees and sawing up wood, and hammering and chiselling. By daybreak, everything was ready.

The Trojans, safe within their city walls, suspected nothing. In the morning, as they had every morning throughout the war, they sharpened their swords and prepared their chariots for another day's gruelling battle.

But this morning, to their surprise, a lookout came running from the city walls with unexpected news. "The Greeks are leaving!" he cried. Everyone rushed to the battlements to see. Sure enough, the Greek ships were sailing away across the silvery sea.

The Trojans opened the gates of their city and rushed down to the shore to watch the ships go. There, they found a surprise waiting for them. Standing on the beach, lit up by the warm glow of the rising sun, stood a giant wooden horse.

The horse was the size of a ship, made from smooth planks that curved gently around its barrel-shaped body. Its neck arched proudly, and its head was carved to look like a powerful warhorse. Inscribed in large lettering along the base were the words, "In return for their safe journey home, the Greeks dedicate this wooden horse to the goddess Athena."

"They've really gone," someone crowed.

"Have they?" asked the Trojan king, Priam, rather more cautiously. "After coming all this way to rescue their queen Helen, it seems strange that they would suddenly give up on her like that?"

Just then there was a shout, and one of his men dragged a cringing, sorry-looking man forward. It was a Greek soldier. "Please don't kill me," the man whined. "They said you would, that you were barbarians and would kill me."

"We are not barbarians!" retorted the king. "What is your name, man? Why didn't you leave with the others?"

"My name is Sinon. They left me behind because I said the gods didn't want us to win," the man said miserably. "They called me a traitor and left me to die at your hands. I hate them. I wish I were a Trojan."

King Priam looked at the man pityingly. "We will not kill you, and you may stay here as a Trojan if you choose," he said. "But tell us. Why did they build this enormous horse?"

The soldiers who held the man released him. Sinon stood a little straighter and smiled nervously at the king. "I suppose they must have thought I was right after all. They built it as an offering to Athena, just as it says, for their safe passage home. They made it this size so that it would be too big to fit through your gates. You see, a prophecy foretold that if you managed to get the horse inside the city walls, Athena would give Troy so much power nobody would ever attack the place again."

He glanced up at the horse. "Maybe you should just burn the thing," he suggested.

"Wait a minute. I don't think it *is* too big to fit inside the gates," said one of the king's men. "It would be a shame not to try if it would keep Troy safe forever."

223

Priam nodded, and ordered the men to take the
wooden horse up to the city. They lashed it with ropes,
and put tree trunks beneath it to act as rollers. Then they
hauled it off the beach and up to the gates of the city.
They hesitated as they approached
the walls – the horse really was huge.
But as they rolled it to the gates,
its ears scraped the top
as it was dragged through.
The gates were just big
enough to allow it inside.

The horse was brought triumphantly inside the city, and everybody cheered.

What a day of celebrations the Trojans had. The women made flower garlands and slung them around the soldiers' necks, and showered the horse with scented petals. Children danced and sang, and the soldiers relaxed for the first time in years, knowing that their city was finally safe. Prince Paris and his beloved Helen, the Greek queen, came out of the palace and joined in the festivities. All day long the party continued, until night finally fell, and the happy Trojans went home to their beds.

Helen was the last to leave. She wandered around the wooden horse alone, trailing her fingers through the petals sprinkled around its base. "This looks like a familiar kind of trickery to me," she murmured, glancing up at the huge belly of the horse. "In fact it wouldn't surprise me one bit," she said a little louder, as if speaking to the horse itself, "if *Odysseus* had a hand in this." Then she added wistfully, "If the Greeks win this war, perhaps it wouldn't be so bad to go back home."

"Helen, are you coming?" Paris called to her from the edge of the city square.

She nodded and ran over to him, and the two walked up to the palace together.

For an hour or two the horse stood silent and alone in the moonlight, in the middle of the sleeping city. Then, in the dead of night, a dark figure crept up to it through the shadows. It was Sinon, the Greek who had been left behind. He reached behind one of its legs, pressed one of the wooden joints, and the entire belly of the horse swung open.

"About time too," a low voice grumbled. "It's really cramped in here." Knotted rope ladders dropped from the horse's gaping belly and down shinned ten, twenty, fifty men or more, clutching their weapons in their teeth. Odysseus climbed down last, and tossed Sinon a sword, "Very convincing," he said admiringly. "We were rather worried when you suggested burning it!"

The Greeks stole through the moonlit square and began their attack. First they killed the guards, who were

226

sleeping off their celebrations. Meanwhile Sinon opened the city gates. During the night, the rest of the Greek army had sailed back to Troy. They were waiting outside, and poured into the city like an unstoppable flood.

By the time the Trojan soldiers came running out, half asleep and fumbling with their weapons, it was too late. Their city fell that very night. King Priam was killed, followed by the remaining members of his family, and many other men besides. Houses were burned and the palace was looted. It wasn't a pretty sight.

Finally, the Greek soldiers found Helen, King Menelaus's stolen queen. Paris, her lover, had already been killed, and when the soldiers broke down the doors of her chamber they found her there alone.

The men fell silent when they saw her, overawed at her remarkable beauty, and at finally meeting this famous woman on whose behalf the entire war had been fought.

Helen stared proudly back at them, until the soldiers remembered themselves and bowed down before her. "Somebody get the king," one of them hissed.

A few moments later, King Menelaus entered the room and gazed at his wife who he had not seen for so long. He hesitated a moment by the door, still unsure whether Helen had been kidnapped by young Paris, or whether she had run away with him of her own free will.

But when Helen held out her hands to him and smiled, Menelaus found he didn't care. She was simply so beautiful, the king was prepared to forgive her anything.

"Come on," he said. "It's time to go home."

The adventures of Odysseus

The goddess Athena gently blew away the clouds. Far below, a ragged fleet of ships was struggling across the sea. "Odysseus is still trying to get home, Father," she said to Zeus.

"Don't you have more important things to think about than the life of one little human?" Zeus asked absently.

Athena sighed. "This one little human helped win the Trojan War with his cunning," she said. "And now he's in danger of being lost at sea."

"That's the life of men for you," said Zeus unsympathetically. "All effort and waste."

"He doesn't deserve it," Athena persisted. "He's been gone ten years already, and he left a wife and a newborn son behind. I think he could do with some help."

"If he's at sea, he's at the mercy of your uncle Poseidon."

"That's what I'm worried about," muttered Athena. "If Poseidon gets into one of his tempers, a single wave of his hand could smash those ships into driftwood."

"Help him if you like, child," Zeus said affectionately, as he peered down over her shoulder. Down below, the ships were drawing near to an island...

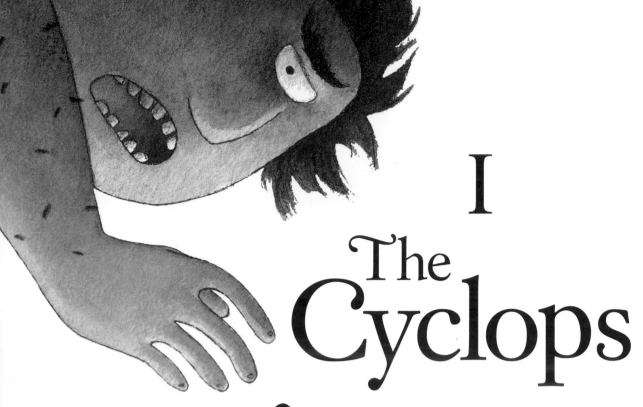

I
The Cyclops

"We'll stop on this island," Odysseus said to his exhausted crew. "There's bound to be some fresh water and food on it somewhere. We can rest here and stock up on provisions for the next leg of the journey home."

They sailed into a quiet, rocky cove and moored their little fleet of ships. It seemed like a pleasant place. The air smelled fresh and birds flitted above the tops of the cliffs, singing sweetly.

"I wonder if anyone lives here," said Odysseus. "Let's explore, and see what we find." He took a large bag of wine from the ship, picked twelve of his crew and set off.

At the top of the cliff, they found a large cave. Odysseus poked his head around the entrance. There was a fireplace in the middle of the floor and lots of empty animal stalls at the back. "Is anyone home?" he called.

There was no answer.

"Look," said one of his men, pointing. On a stone slab near the fireplace was a row of giant bowls of milk, and several large rounds of cheese. The men were ravenous, having run out of food a few days ago. Before Odysseus could stop them, they had piled into the cave and were sharing out huge hunks of cheese. "Whoever lives here surely wouldn't deny us a bite to eat," said one of the men with his mouth full.

Odysseus shrugged. "I suppose we can offer to pay for the food when the owner returns," he said, and sat down to wait.

A little while later, they heard footsteps outside. A flock of sheep and goats entered the cave first, jostling past the men and into the empty stalls. Then a shadow fell across the cave opening. It was a very, very large shadow. Odysseus stood up to greet its owner.

An enormous, ugly giant came inside. He was barrel-chested and muscular, with a single, bulging eye right in the middle of his forehead. Odysseus immediately recognized him from tales he had heard as a boy. He was a cyclops.

The cyclops ushered the last couple of goats inside before rolling an enormous boulder across the entrance of the cave to close it. Then he turned and saw Odysseus and his men.

While the rest of the men sat gaping, Odysseus smiled politely at the cyclops. "Please excuse our intrusion," he said smoothly. "We're on our way home from fighting in the Trojan War."

231

The cyclops peered down at them and grinned broadly. "Dinner," he said.

Odysseus nodded. "Yes indeed. Your cheese is so delicious my men just couldn't resist–" He stopped mid-sentence as the giant reached over, picked up two of the men and crammed them, whole, into his mouth.

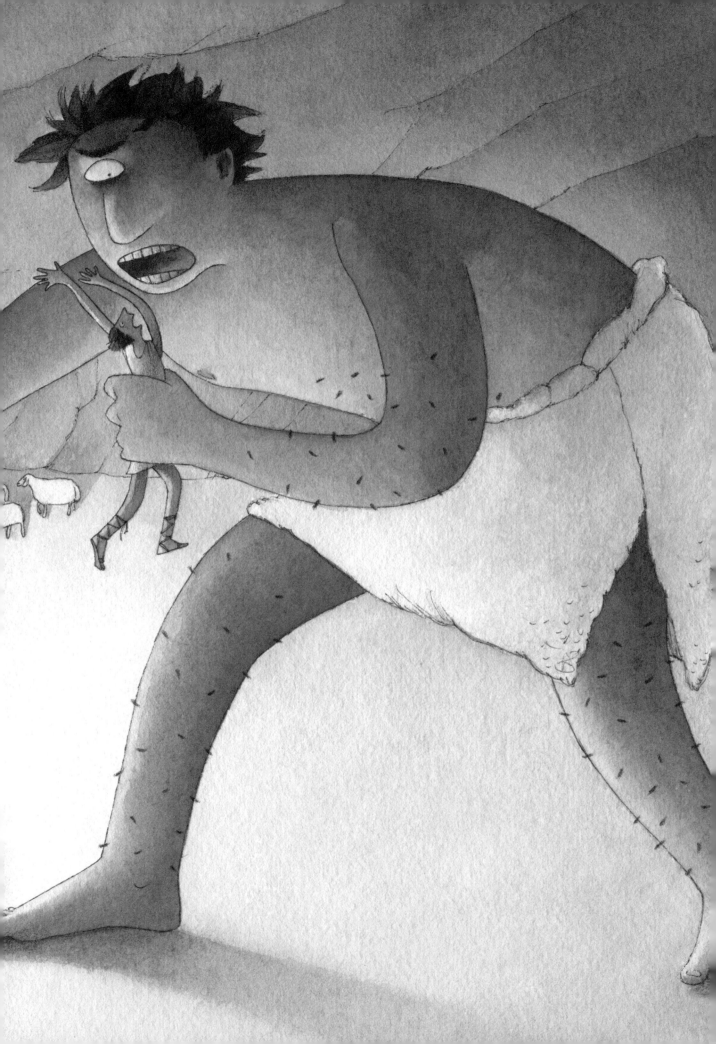

Shrieking with terror, the rest of the men ran for their lives, knocking over bowls of milk and tripping over one another in their panic. The cyclops caught another man by one leg and dangled him in the air like a juicy grape. He swallowed the first two and then lowered his third, sobbing victim into his mouth. The man's cries quickly fell silent as the cyclops began to chew.

Odysseus and his men cowered in the back of the cave while the cyclops calmly stoked up his fire and made himself comfortable. Eventually one man whispered. "Captain, we have to kill the cyclops before he eats any more of us."

"No," replied Odysseus quickly. "Think about it. We'd never be able to roll the boulder from the entrance ourselves. It's far too heavy. We'd starve to death in here."

"Then what?" The man's voice was hoarse with fear.

"I'll think of something," promised Odysseus, and he racked his brains for a plan.

The cyclops was relaxing by the fire, using a thin branch to pick the bits from between his teeth. Clutching the big bag of wine he'd brought from the ship, Odysseus stood up and walked over to the cyclops.

"It seems we've started off on the wrong foot," he said in a friendly tone.

The cyclops raised his single eyebrow and stared down at him.

"I have some fine wine here," Odysseus continued. "Perhaps you'd like a drop or two to wash down your – er – your meal."

The cyclops held out a bowl, and Odysseus filled it with wine. The cyclops knocked it back and held out the bowl for more. Odysseus filled it again. "What is your name?" the giant asked between gulps of wine.

"My name is Nobody," answered Odysseus, emptying the last of the wine into the giant's bowl.

The cyclops drank it, tipping the bowl upside down and slurping the last dregs from the bottom. "I give you present for wine," he slurred, leering down at Odysseus. "I eat you last." He burst out laughing, blasting Odysseus with his foul-smelling breath. Odysseus pressed his lips together in a grim smile and said nothing.

The strength of the wine was taking effect, and the cyclops suddenly dropped his bowl and slumped down onto his side. Almost immediately, he began to snore.

Odysseus crept back to his men, and whispered the rest of his plan to them.

Quickly and quietly, the men leaped into action. They scurried up to the fireside and, together, helped him lift up the cyclops's enormous walking staff. They held the tip in the fire. Then, on Odysseus's command, they charged at the sleeping giant with the staff, and plunged its burning tip deep into his eye.

It sizzled horribly and the cyclops woke up howling. Everyone scrambled for safety as he thrashed around in agony, trying to pluck the staff from his eye. He threw it down and covered his eye, still wailing. His cries were so loud they must have carried across the entire island. Before long, hurried footsteps could be heard outside.

"Brother, are you alright in there?" boomed a voice.

"Nobody hurt me!" answered the cyclops.

"Oh good," said the voice.

"Nobody HURT me!" the cyclops repeated indignantly. "Nobody is here in my cave!"

"All right, all right," said the voice. "We heard you the first time." Odysseus smiled to himself; his plan had worked. He and his men listened with relief as the footsteps faded away into the distance again.

The cyclops began to fumble blindly around the cave, muttering menacingly. "I eat you all," he threatened. The men dodged out of the way of his groping hands until, eventually, he gave up trying to find them. He lay down again and went to sleep.

When morning came, the sheep trotted out of their stalls and gathered at the front of the cave. The cyclops rolled the boulder a little way away from the mouth of the cave to let them out to pasture. But he sat to one side of the narrow gap and felt everything that walked past him, to make sure that none of the men escaped.

Luckily, Odysseus had guessed that might happen and had prepared everyone. During the night, he and his men had twisted straw from the stalls to make rope, and used it to tie the strongest rams together in groups of three. Now, they clung to the undersides of the rams, their fists buried in their long fleeces. As the rams trotted out of the cave, the cyclops felt their shaggy backs and heads and let them pass. The men all made it out of the cave without the cyclops suspecting a thing.

Outside, the men dropped to the ground. Without a word between them, they drove the sheep and goats down the rocky path to the ships. Only when they had set sail, and were leaving the island behind them did Odysseus break their silence. He shouted up to the cyclops on the cliff outside his cave. "We've escaped, you filthy man-eater!" he shouted. "I just wanted you to know."

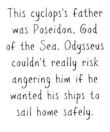

Enraged, the cyclops tore a rock from the cliff and hurled it in the direction of Odysseus's voice. It splashed into the sea, narrowly missing the ship but casting large waves over the side.

"Stop shouting at him, Captain," begged one of his crew. "We don't want to have escaped the cyclops only to have him sink us."

This cyclops's father was Poseidon, God of the Sea. Odysseus couldn't really risk angering him if he wanted his ships to sail home safely.

But Odysseus hadn't finished yet. His defiance was fired by grief at the grisly deaths of his three men. "I want you to know who blinded you, so you can tell anyone who asks," he shouted. "My true name is Odysseus. Do you hear me?"

"I hear you," roared the cyclops, hurling another rock after them. "My father will punish you for this, Odysseus!"

Odysseus went to the front of his ship and led the little fleet back out to sea.

II The bag of winds

Odysseus and his crew sailed their ships across the stormy sea. They were completely at the mercy of the crashing waves. "If only we could keep to our course," said Odysseus through gritted teeth, "we might finally make it home. The way we're being thrown around, we could end up anywhere." The men strained at the oars, but it was all they could do to stop the boats from capsizing.

Finally, after five days of constant struggle, the storm broke. The waves subsided and the crew collapsed over their oars, drenched to the skin and exhausted.

Odysseus had no idea where in the world they could be. In the blissfully calm light of dawn, he suddenly spied a small island ahead of them. Strangely, it appeared to be moving, just like their boats, on the swell of the waves. "How odd," he murmured.

They drifted closer, and a grand palace came into view. The building perfectly reflected the sky, so at that moment it was rose-red like the dawn with white cloud shapes moving very slowly across its surface. This strange quality made it almost impossible to see the palace from even a small distance away.

As they drew up to the island, a bearded man in storm-blue robes came out to greet them. "Welcome, tired sailors," he said warmly. "The King of the Winds at your service. Please moor your boats and come ashore."

"Thank you," replied Odysseus. He hopped onto the island and was surprised to find that the ground rippled gently beneath his feet. The King of the Winds smiled at his guest. "This is a floating island," he explained. "I don't need my island to be anchored against the winds, since it is I who command them."

He gestured for the men to come with him. "Perhaps our luck is turning," Odysseus thought as they left their boats and followed the king inland.

The palace was beautiful. It had tiny cloud-like swirls of sculpted detail all over the walls and doors. "The winds can do some marvellous things," said the king, when he saw Odysseus admiring the patterns. "You look weary. Please come in."

Inside, the men were received by servants who showed them where they could wash and gave them clean clothes to wear. Once they were ready, they sat down with the king to a fine dinner, and Odysseus told him all about their adventures so far.

"You sound like a brave man," said the king when Odysseus had finished his story.

"And I like helping people who deserve it. Tomorrow I will send you on your way with the winds on your side."

In the morning, while the men were taking some generous gifts of food and wine down to the ships, the king took Odysseus aside. He handed him a large, heavy bag, tied tightly at the neck. "I am entrusting you with this," he said gravely. "All of the winds are imprisoned in this bag, save one. The West Wind is still free, and I have commanded it to blow you swiftly home. Promise me that once your ships are moored safely on your home shore – and not a moment sooner – you will untie the bag and let loose the winds."

"I promise," said Odysseus. He thanked the king warmly for his help and stowed the bag in the back of his ship. As soon as they unfurled their sails, the gentle West Wind puffed into them, and the fleet continued on its journey. The floating island shrank into the distance as their ships sped faster and faster across the calm sea.

After all this time, they were finally going home, and none of the men even had to lift a finger.

Odysseus lay down in the back of his ship and closed his eyes. With a peaceful sigh, he slipped into a happy slumber, filled with dreams of his wife and son.

In the front of the ship, the men fell to talking. "I can't wait to see my sweetheart," said one of the younger men. "It's been so long she'll scarcely recognize me."

"Aye and my children," said an older man.

"We've not got much to show for our troubles and all our time away, have we?" muttered another.

"Plenty of aches and pains and a few extra years on our faces," a fourth snorted. "Did you see that huge bag Odysseus got from the king? I wonder what was in it."

"Some treasure he's keeping for himself, no doubt," grumbled the first man. "We've done just as much as he has. He ought to share everything with us."

Suddenly, the lookout gave an excited gasp. "There!" he cried, pointing at the horizon. "Isn't that Ithaca up ahead? We're almost home!"

They all turned to stare at the three-peaked island in the distance. Ithaca. It was unmistakable. They gazed in silence for a few moments, each man lost in sweet expectation of their homecoming.

Then one man broke the silence. "Let's just have a quick look in that bag, before we wake Odysseus. There might be something nice inside that we can take to our families; a little fair payment for following the captain around for so long."

He crept past Odysseus, rummaged around in the back of the ship and came back with the bag. He was staggering slightly under its weight. "There must be loads of goodies in here," he said. "What do you reckon?"

The others agreed. And so, in sight of their longed-for homeland, while their captain slept, they opened up the bag of winds.

There was a deafening noise, and the North Wind burst out of the bag. It blasted the man who'd opened the bag high into the air, and he plummeted into the sea about a mile away from the ship.

Then the North Wind slammed
into the ship's mast, snapping it in two
and knocking another four men into the sea.
The other winds writhed out of the bag after it,
blowing men over, ripping the ship's rails to pieces,
and plunging into the sea with such force that a tidal
wave rose up and crashed over the deck.

"What on earth is going on?" shouted Odysseus,
torn from sleep by the commotion and making his way
down the ship. But no one heard him above the din.

The deck lurched and a man slid past, wailing
helplessly. Odysseus sprang forward and caught his
wrist before he fell overboard, wrenching him to safety.
"Hold onto this," he said, wrapping the panicked man's
arms around the mast.

All around him, wood was splintering, ropes were
snapping and screaming men were falling overboard,
their heads and flailing arms being sucked beneath
the foaming waves. It was complete chaos.

The sail was still flapping around, half-filled
with wind, although the mast had fallen.
If Odysseus didn't do something quickly,
it was going to drag the ship over. "Untie
that rope!" he ordered another sailor.
"We have to take down the sail!"

He set to work, chivvying fear-numbed sailors into action, lashing down the loose ropes and planks, and doing everything in his power to hold his ship and crew together. Meanwhile winds hurled and surged, sweeping the ship back in the direction they had come.

By the time the winds dispersed hours later, all that was left of the entire fleet was Odysseus's single, broken ship. All around them was empty sea – Ithaca was nowhere to be seen. Odysseus buried his face in his hands in despair.

A half-drowned sailor, still clinging to the mast, spoke up in a trembling voice. "Land ahoy, Captain."

Odysseus looked up to see an island ahead. It seemed to be moving, like a ship, on the swell of the waves; on it stood a palace whose walls reflected the stormy sky. They were right back where they'd started.

As they drifted closer to the island, the King of the Winds appeared. "I told you not to open the bag until you were home," he barked. "What kind of an idiot are you?"

"We were within sight of home," Odysseus answered, "when one of my crew opened the bag. I'm sure it was a mistake. Please could you help us again?"

"No," snapped the King of the Winds. "You don't deserve any more help. Besides, it's obvious you're cursed, and I'm not going against the will of the gods." He called up the winds, which gathered around the floating island and propelled it away across the water.

Odysseus watched as the island shrank from view, leaving him, the remains of his crew and their broken ship alone in the middle of the inky sea.

243

III
Circe
the
sorceress

Having lost all the other ships in their fleet, Odysseus and his crew sailed on numb with grief. They had been blown so far from their course, they had no idea where they were. But there was nothing else to do but to carry on sailing across the empty sea.

Eventually, one day, they came to a golden shore. They dragged their boat up the beach, lay down wearily on the sand beside it and slept.

The next morning, Odysseus roused them. "Come," he said. "One way or another, we have managed to survive. We should have a look for water and supplies, and then be on our way."

"What's the point?" muttered one of the men.

"If we give up hope, we'll never get home," Odysseus urged. "Come along. Who knows what we might find here."

"We might find man-eating monsters," said another man fearfully.

The others murmured in agreement.

"Or a kind-hearted sage who can tell us the way home," Odysseus countered. "We don't know until we try."

After a little more discussion, the men decided to split into two parties. They drew straws to decide who would explore which area of the island. Odysseus's group would search along the shore for fruit and fresh water, and to look after the boat. The other group would head inland. "Keep your wits about you," Odysseus advised Eurylochus, the leader of the other group. "We'll meet you back at the ship at noon."

Eurylochus and his men set off into the trees. After a walk through the forest, they stumbled out into a sunlit glade, in the middle of which stood a palace. To their horror, the palace was surrounded by fierce-looking beasts — flint-eyed wolves, muscular lions and huge black bears.

When the animals caught sight of the men, they began running at them. The men backed away on trembling legs. But then they realized the animals weren't coming to harm them. The wolves wagged their tails like dogs; the bears lay down at their feet; and the lions rubbed against them like friendly, oversized cats.

The sailors stared at one another nervously, wondering what this strange way of behaving could mean.

Just then, they heard singing coming from within the palace. It was a woman's voice, warm and melodic. "What a beautiful sound," said one of the men. "I think we're in luck. That's no ogre ready to turn us away or eat us." He called out, "Hello there! There are some weary sailors calling at your door."

Almost at once, a woman opened the doors of the palace. She radiated beauty like the sun, with shining golden hair that cascaded almost to the floor. Smiling, she beckoned them over. "Don't worry," she said, gesturing to the animals, "they won't harm you." The men gathered around her like moths to a flame. "My name is Circe," she said. "Why don't you all come inside?"

The men followed her inside. All of them, that is, apart from Eurylochus. Something about the situation made him feel uneasy, and so he dropped to the back of the group. As the others filed through the door, he slipped away and went to the side of the palace, where he could watch what happened through a window.

Inside, Circe said to the sailors. "You look as though you're in need of a good meal."

"Oh yes, please," they chorused.

She showed them through to her dining hall, where a table was laid with the kinds of rich food the men had only dreamed of since they had left home. There was creamy soft cheese and sweet honey, and barley bread and tender, juicy meat. The men fell upon the feast and began stuffing themselves.

Very quickly, something very odd began to happen. Their bellies grew round and their shoulders hunched over. Their noses got wider and flatter. Their skin sprouted bristles and their ears grew floppy, and curly tails sprouted from their backsides. Soon, they could do nothing but grunt and squeal in alarm at one another.

They had turned into pigs.

IV Mysteries and dangers at sea

"Come to us," the sirens sang, "and we'll tell you a secret for you alone." The creatures sat high on the treacherous rocks, shimmering strangely in the pale dawn light. Odysseus gazed at them from his ship, squinting against the dazzling glare. He longed to go closer, but he knew he shouldn't.

Everyone knew the stories of sailors being lured to their deaths by the sirens, and Odysseus was no fool. Before they got to where the sirens lived, he'd asked his crew to plug their ears with beeswax so they couldn't hear a thing. He had also asked them to tie him to the mast.

He wanted to hear the sirens' famous voices, so he'd left his own ears unplugged. Although he thought it unlikely that anything could lure him to his death when he was so desperate to get home, he decided he'd better take precautions. It was just as well. The sirens' voices filled him with such desperate longing that he would have gladly thrown himself overboard to reach them.

The ship eased slowly past the shimmering creatures. The sharp rocks beneath them were littered with the grisly remains of ships and sailors who had succumbed to their charms.

The sirens brushed back their hair from their pretty faces and beckoned to Odysseus. They looked so sweet and sad that he felt his heart wrench in his chest. "Leave us now and you'll never know," they sang. "It is only you we can give our secret to..."

All thoughts of reaching home were driven from his head. "Leave me here," he begged his unhearing crew, struggling to free himself. "Untie me!" he ordered the nearest sailor.

The man understood him well enough, despite being unable to hear. He shook his head nervously and tightened the ropes instead. "Sorry, Captain," he mumbled. "Just following your orders." The rest kept on rowing.

Only when they had long passed the rocks, did his men unplug their ears and untie their captain. With the singing out of earshot, Odysseus returned to his old self. "I was completely enchanted," he confessed. "Nothing else mattered to me – not even staying alive."

"You're the only person ever to have heard them and lived," remarked one of his crew.

"If we make it home for me to tell the tale," Odysseus said grimly, "I'll be a happy man. But there are many dangers ahead of us yet. Look." He nodded ahead to where, in the distance, a huge plume of water was shooting out of the sea.

"Charybdis," the old helmsman murmured under his breath. The younger sailors looked puzzled, so he explained. "She's a giant whirlpool that sucks everything that passes near her down under the water, and then spits it back out whenever she pleases. Ships that go under can disappear for months. When they come back up they look as if they've been chewed by a monster."

As they approached, the helmsman steered the ship away from the whirlpool over to the smooth cliffs to one side. Although safely beyond its pull, the men shuddered as they watched the foamy water being sucked down into a dark funnel in the middle.

Odysseus, meanwhile, was staring at the cliff on the other side. He'd noticed a cave halfway up, and something inside that cave was moving. He could just about see the gleam of eyes in the shadows. Whatever it was, it was watching them.

As they drew nearer, a head emerged on a long, sinuous neck. Its narrow eyes were fixed on the ship. Another head appeared, and another, and another, and then the creature's scaly, muscled body. It gripped the cliff and strained its six necks towards the ship. It was Scylla, a monster known to have a taste for human flesh.

"Turn away!" someone shrieked as all six sets of jaws snapped open to reveal rows of dagger-like teeth. The helmsman hurriedly steered away from the cliffs. But, almost immediately, they felt themselves being dragged into the whirling vortex on the other side.

"Turn back!" Odysseus shouted. All the men fell on their oars and began to row, and the helmsman had no choice but to steer back in the direction of the monster.

It lunged and seized three men from the ship. "Captain, save us!" they cried. But Odysseus could only watch aghast as they disappeared down three of Scylla's throats.

All the men had dropped their oars and were cowering on the far side of the ship. Without anyone rowing, the vessel began to be sucked into the whirlpool again. Odysseus flung himself over to the empty side and began tugging at an oar. "Sit down and help me row!" he ordered his men. They were staring into the eye of the whirlpool, frozen to the spot with fear.

"Help me row!" Odysseus shouted again. "It's our only hope!" This time, the crew threw themselves down and began rowing with all their might. The monster lunged again and three more men were plucked screaming from among them. Sweating with terror, the others gritted their teeth and kept on rowing.

Slowly, the ship drew out of Scylla's reach. The pull of the whirlpool grew weaker and weaker, until finally the ship was clear of danger. The remaining sailors slumped to the deck and wept.

A gentle breeze swelled, and they sailed on a while in sorrowful silence. Then the lookout cried, "Land ahoy!" They had reached an island. It looked welcoming and calm. White cattle grazed on lush green grass or lay peacefully in the sun.

They sailed into shore and dragged their ship up the sandy beach. Now they were closer, Odysseus realized that the cattle weren't ordinary animals. They were so white they almost glowed, and they had doe-like eyes and twisted golden horns. "These are the sun god's cattle," he told his men. "I've heard about them — they're supposed to be immortal."

"They look tasty to me," said a sailor.

"We have enough with us to eat," Odysseus said. "Promise me that none of you will harm these cattle. They belong to a god. It would be a crime."

"It's a crime to gnaw on stale bread," the sailor grumbled, "when we could be turning these cattle into juicy steaks," But Odysseus insisted. Eventually every man gave his word to leave the cattle alone.

The sun god, Helios, kept a herd of 350 immortal cattle and the same number of immortal sheep on the island. There was no way they could have come to harm without Helios finding out. He was all-seeing and all-hearing, and his two daughters lived on the island to watch over the animals.

They set up camp in a meadow overlooking the beach, built a fire and slept soundly beneath the stars. In the morning, they were woken by torrential rain. The sky was purple and the sea was rough and stormy. As the day went on, the rain cleared, but the wind whipped the sea into such a frenzy that they decided to wait out the storm before setting sail.

However, when the storm calmed the following day, the wind was blowing due south. Home lay to the north-east, so there was no point in setting sail. The following week, the wind changed to due west. An entire month went by, and their provisions were running low, but the winds continued to blow in the wrong directions.

One afternoon, Odysseus was dozing in his tent.

He was dreaming of a fine homecoming feast and awoke in some confusion to the smell of roasting meat and laughter. His heart sank when he realized it wasn't a dream.

Down on the beach, he found his men gathered around a large fire. They had roasted an entire bull and were stuffing themselves with meat.

"What are you doing?" he shouted. "You promised not to harm these creatures. The gods will certainly punish us for this. We're doomed!"

"We were doomed anyway," said one man guiltily. "We can't get home and our food's running out. At least this way we won't starve to death."

Then he groaned and clutched his stomach. At the same time, another pointed at the meat on the spit with a cry of disgust, "Look," he wailed. "It's moving."

It was true. The cattle were immortal and that meant that even their flesh could not die. The skinned hides began to crawl across the ground and the meat started writhing on the spits. "Make offerings to all the gods immediately," said Odysseus. "Beg them to spare us."

The next morning dawned calm and clear, with a steady easterly wind. Odysseus eyed the sky suspiciously. "I had expected a storm," he said.

"Perhaps the gods don't mind us eating their cattle after all," said one sailor. "What else are they good for?"

Odysseus shrugged warily, "Still," he said, "we'd better set sail while we can."

They set about packing up the ship. Before noon, they were out at sea. They sailed on tranquil water until they were hours from shore. Then, suddenly, the weather turned. Clouds towered like furious giants above them. Thunder rolled and lightning flashed, and the sea heaved and churned. Colossal waves rose up and smashed onto the deck like angry fists.

Odysseus struggled to take down the sail, but before he could untie the ropes, lightning struck the mast and it fell, dragging the entire ship over to one side. Several men slid helplessly into the swirling water and their bobbing heads disappeared beneath the waves.

Odysseus wrestled in vain with the base of the fallen mast, trying to release it so that the ship would not capsize. Eventually he gave up. Nobody could hear him shouting for help above the howling wind, and he could barely see for the lashing rain. The ship was half capsized and lurching around so much that it was all anyone could do to hold on.

All around him, men were being thrown overboard. In desperation, Odysseus found some rope and strapped himself to a splintered wooden plank. He held on to his ship's rail as the boat was torn plank from sorry plank by the waves, and all his men were lost.

In the end Odysseus, too, was pulled into the angry sea. The waves threw him around cruelly, as if they had been sent deliberately to punish him. Time and time again, he was plunged underwater, but his wooden plank always bobbed back up to the surface. Finally, half drowned and soundly beaten, Odysseus lost consciousness.

He woke up lying sprawled on his front.

But he was too exhausted to open his eyes, and for a moment he wasn't sure whether he was alive or dead. He could hear the lap of the waves on the shore, and a bird's sharp cry above him. Then he noticed the smell in the air. Beyond the tang of sea salt, was the scent of pine. It smelled like just like the trees back home.

He opened his eyes. Beneath him, there were hundreds and hundreds of smooth, white pebbles, like those he used to skim across the water as a boy while dreaming of adventures out to sea.

Slowly, Odysseus sat up. As he looked around, tears sprang into his eyes. "I've heard the sirens' dizzying song, tasted enchanted food and met dazzling goddesses," he murmured hoarsely, "but nothing has ever sounded, smelled or looked sweeter to me than this. Thank all the gods – I'm home."

"You might well thank the gods, stranger," said a voice nearby. "They could easily have drowned you."

A young shepherd boy was standing behind Odysseus, watching him with clear, sky-blue eyes. The boy helped him to his feet, and Odysseus studied his face as he did so. There was a powerful radiance about him that Odysseus recognized. "I'm very grateful," he said quietly.

Before his eyes, the boy transformed. His limbs lengthened, his face softened, and his hair spread glossily around his shoulders. In a moment, he had become a tall, powerful-looking woman. "Athena," Odysseus breathed.

She smiled. "I should have known never to try to trick a trickster. You saw through my disguise," she said. "Odysseus, your journey is over. Your wife, Penelope, is waiting for you," she said, "and a fine, grown-up son too."

"I only hope they recognize me," Odysseus said with a rueful smile. "I've been gone nineteen long years." The war, his hard journey and all the years he'd been struggling to get home had changed him — he felt like an old man.

"I'll make sure they do," Athena said. She lightly touched his shoulders, and all the pain and stiffness flowed out of his body. Suddenly, he felt younger than he had in years. "Your son is a brave young man now," Athena told him. "And although your wife had many offers of marriage from suitors eager to take your place, she refused them all. She never stopped believing you would come back to her. So go and find them, Odysseus, and be happy. Welcome home," Athena said, and she vanished into thin air.

Odysseus, his heart so full of joy he could scarcely breathe, turned away from the sea and headed up the coastal path home.

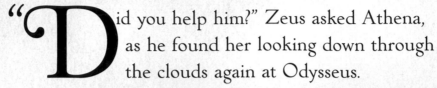

"id you help him?" Zeus asked Athena, as he found her looking down through the clouds again at Odysseus.

"Only where he really needed it," she replied. "Look – he's back home now. There he is, on that little island he loves so much. He's hugging his wife Penelope and tousling his son's hair – they're laughing. He's been gone so long, his son is as tall as he is now."

"How quickly the lives of men pass," Zeus remarked. "Nineteen years have gone by in the blink of an eye. Come now. We've more interesting things to tend to than the fate of men."

Athena gave one last look before drawing the clouds together. "Goodbye brave Odysseus," she murmured. "May your wits continue to protect you where I do not."

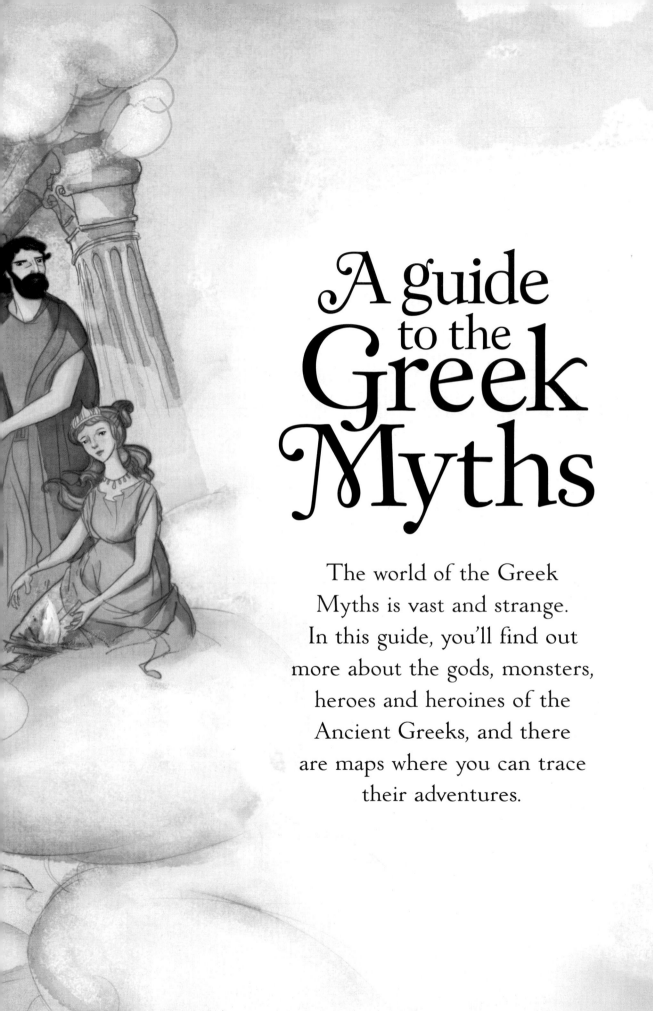

A guide
to the
Greek
Myths

The world of the Greek
Myths is vast and strange.
In this guide, you'll find out
more about the gods, monsters,
heroes and heroines of the
Ancient Greeks, and there
are maps where you can trace
their adventures.

Who's who
in the
Greek Myths?

The following pages list all the characters
(and some places) that appear in the stories in this book,
as well as some that you may come across elsewhere.

The characters are grouped by type, such as gods,
monsters and people. Their entries describe what they did,
and how they were related to other characters and stories
in the Greek Myths. Names written in *italics* have their
own entries. You can find the page numbers for every
entry in the index on pages 302-304.

The first beings

Before the beginning of the world, there was just empty
nothingness, known as Chaos. But then, the universe began
to take shape, and the first beings appeared.

Gaia

The very first being to burst into existence out of Chaos. Also known
as Mother Earth, Gaia had countless children, including various types
of giants. Once she had raised them, she fell into a deep sleep and
became the *earth*.

Some of the names in Greek mythology can be difficult to say.
To hear these names read out loud, go to the Usborne Quicklinks website at
www.usborne-quicklinks.com and enter the key words "Greek Myths".

Uranus

Lord of the sky. He appeared shortly after *Gaia*, and they had lots of children together. But, setting a pattern for many gods who came after him, Uranus was a terrible parent. He was repulsed by some of his children, and imprisoned them inside *Gaia*. She turned against him and encouraged their other children to rebel. As a result, Uranus was defeated by his son, *Cronus*, who then took his place as ruler of the universe.

Uranus was lord of the sky and ruled the universe for a while.

Other early beings

Almost as soon as *Gaia* and *Uranus* came into existence, a whole host of other beings followed. Each of them stood for a different aspect of life, the universe and everything else. Here are a few of them:

Erebus
The shadows of night, husband of *Nyx*.

Hemera
Nyx's daughter, the day.

Eris
The spirit of strife.

Aether
The air of the upper sky.

She loved bloodshed and trouble, and is said to have helped to cause the Trojan War.

Nike
The spirit of victory.

Hypnos
The lord of sleep.

Thanatos
Peaceful death, the twin brother of *Hypnos*.

Nyx
The night itself, mother of *Charon*.

She drove a night-black chariot across the sky to bring the darkness at the end of every day.

Titans and giants

Together, *Gaia* and *Uranus* had some truly huge children: the titans, the *cyclops* and the *hundred-handers*. The first titans were godlike giants who overthrew *Uranus* and ruled the world until they, in turn, were overthrown by *Zeus*. There were twelve of them:

Cronus
Head titan, father of *Demeter*, *Hestia*, *Hera*, *Hades*, *Poseidon* and *Zeus*. He knew one of his children would depose him, so he swallowed them all... except *Zeus*, who freed his siblings and defeated Cronus.

Rhea

Cyclops

Hyperion
Crius
Coeus
Iapetos

Some say these titans helped Cronus to overthrow Uranus.

Oceanus
Tethys

Water giants who fathered thousands of water nymphs.

Rhea
Wife of *Cronus*. She tricked him into swallowing a stone instead of his son, *Zeus*.

Mnemosyne
In charge of memory, and mother of the *Muses*.

Themis
In charge of justice, law and order, and mother of the *Fates*.

Theia
Wife of *Hyperion*.

Phoebe
Wife of *Coeus*.

Cyclops and the Hundred-handers

The younger brothers of the titans, these ugly giants had looks only their mother, *Gaia*, could love. Each cyclops had only one eye; their siblings, the hundred-handers, each had a hundred hands and fifty heads. They were all imprisoned by their father, *Cronus*, but later freed by the mighty *Zeus*.

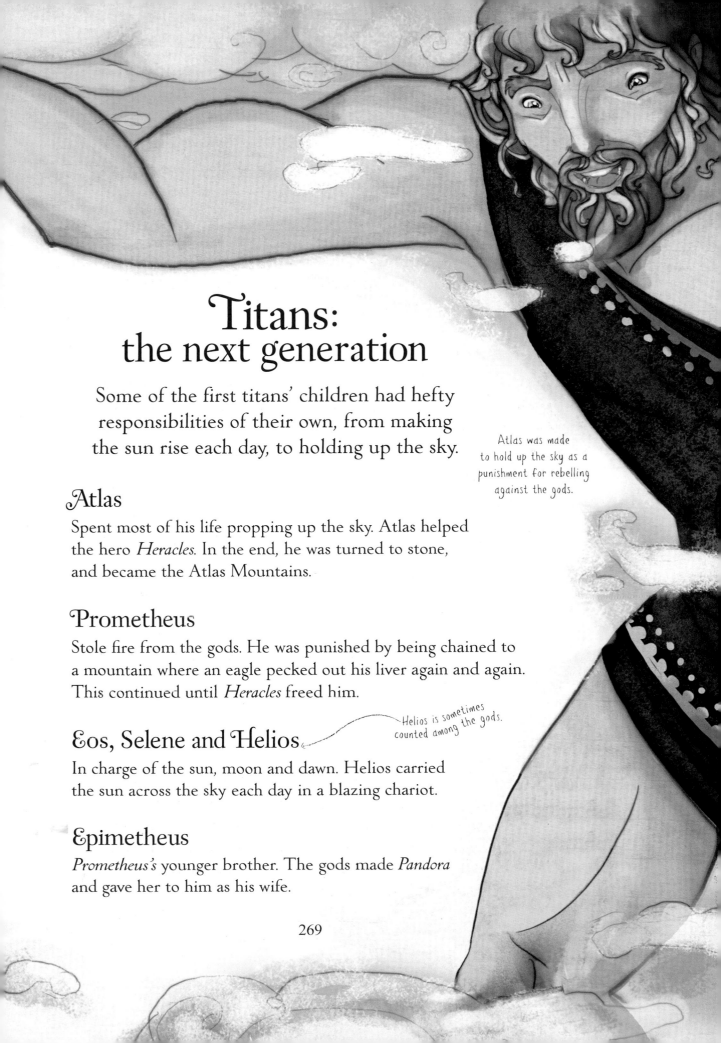

Titans: the next generation

Some of the first titans' children had hefty responsibilities of their own, from making the sun rise each day, to holding up the sky.

Atlas was made to hold up the sky as a punishment for rebelling against the gods.

Atlas

Spent most of his life propping up the sky. Atlas helped the hero *Heracles*. In the end, he was turned to stone, and became the Atlas Mountains.

Prometheus

Stole fire from the gods. He was punished by being chained to a mountain where an eagle pecked out his liver again and again. This continued until *Heracles* freed him.

Eos, Selene and Helios

Helios is sometimes counted among the gods.

In charge of the sun, moon and dawn. Helios carried the sun across the sky each day in a blazing chariot.

Epimetheus

Prometheus's younger brother. The gods made *Pandora* and gave her to him as his wife.

The first gods

All the first gods were children of *Rhea* and *Cronus*, apart from *Aphrodite*, whose father was *Uranus*. The *cyclops* built these gods a grand palace in the clouds above the world's tallest mountain – Mount Olympus. It was called *Olympus*, so the gods who lived there are often known as the Olympian gods.

Zeus

The mighty king of the gods. As a baby, he narrowly escaped being swallowed by his father, *Cronus*. All the same, he managed to grow up safe, sound and very strong. Zeus later defeated *Cronus*, took over as ruler of the universe, and freed the *cyclops* and the *hundred-handers*. In return, they gave him a set of magical thunderbolts, which he often hurled at mortals when he felt angry.

Hera

Zeus's wife, queen of the gods, and goddess of marriage and childbirth. Petty and jealous by nature, Hera made life very difficult for *Heracles*, who was *Zeus's* son by a human woman. She did help some humans, though, and watched over the hero *Jason*. Hera had four children with *Zeus: Ares, Hebe, Eileithyia* and *Hephaestus*.

The great god Zeus watched over the lives of mortals down on earth – and occasionally made their lives rather difficult.

Poseidon

God of the sea. He carried a fork-like weapon known as a trident, which he used to stir up the waves and create storms at sea. Sailors prayed to him if they had a long voyage ahead, hoping he would help them to arrive safe and shipshape. As he rode in his chariot through the sea, he was often accompanied by beautiful sea *nymphs*.

Hestia

A rare type of god – a nice one. At least, she didn't delight in meddling with the lives of humans, unlike most other gods. Hestia never had children, got married or had love affairs, either. As the goddess of hearth and home, she preferred a quiet life.

Demeter

Goddess of nature. When her daughter, *Persephone*, was kidnapped by *Hades*, Demeter was so upset that she neglected her duties, causing leaves and flowers to wither and die. Eventually, it was arranged that *Persephone* would spend half the year with *Hades* and the other half with Demeter. This was how the seasons came to be.

Aphrodite

Hades

God of the *Underworld* and ruler of the dead who took *Demeter's* daughter, *Persephone*, to be his queen. He was a wealthy god, as he lived underground, which meant he owned all the gold and gems that can be found in the earth

Aphrodite

Goddess of love. She was born when drops of *Uranus's* blood fell in the sea. Aphrodite had the power to make the course of true love run smooth but, if you crossed her, she could make it very bumpy indeed. Although she was the wife of *Hephaestus*, she fell in love with *Ares*, with whom she had a son, *Eros*.

Zeus's godly offspring

If having children were a competitive sport, *Zeus* would be the world champion. Here are just a few of his most famous children, who were all gods themselves.

Athena

Warrior goddess Athena was always ready for a battle and seldom seen without her helmet on.

Goddess of wisdom, war and weaving. Athena chose not to have children, and her own birth was very strange — she was born out of *Zeus's* head. She not only sprang out fully grown, but also fully armed and shouting a ferocious battle cry.

Artemis

The goddess of all sorts of things, from hunting and wild animals, to the moon and young girls. Her mother was a moon goddess and her twin brother was the god *Apollo*. Artemis was another goddess who swore never to marry or have children.

Apollo

The god of music, art, sunlight, and telling the future. Apollo was the best musician in the universe, and didn't take kindly to those who suggested otherwise.

Hephaestus

The blacksmith god. He made weapons for the other gods and married *Aphrodite*. Hephaestus was thrown out of *Olympus* because he was physically weak.

Ares

Another war god. Ironically, Ares was wasn't very good at winning fights – in one battle, *Athena* beat him easily. He also backed the losing side in the Trojan War.

Hermes

Messenger to the gods who flew on winged sandals. He could be a troublemaker, but he could be helpful too, carrying messages from the gods to mortals, and performing heroic rescues.

Hebe

Goddess who served wine to the other gods. She was put out of a job by a beautiful mortal named *Ganymede*. But she married the dashing hero *Heracles*, which must have softened the blow.

Dionysus

The god of wine. He and his fun-loving followers, various *nymphs* and *satyrs*, could always be relied on to get a party started.

Persephone

Demeter's daughter. She was kidnapped by *Hades*, and taken to the Underworld, where she ate six pomegranate seeds. After that, she had to spend six months of every year as queen of the *Underworld*.

Eileithyia

Goddess of childbirth. Eileithyia could help women in childbirth, or make it more difficult for them.

Eros

God of love. With his magic arrows, *Zeus's* winged grandson Eros could make people fall in love. But he wasn't immune to love himself, and fell for a beautiful human woman named *Psyche*.

Nature gods and spirits

The natural world had many gods and spirits, from mighty *wind gods* to hairy, drunken oafs called *satyrs*.

Wind gods

Four gods, each linked to a point of the compass and a season. Zephyrus, the West Wind, brought the spring; Notus, the South Wind, was linked to the summer; Eurus, the East Wind blew the leaves from the trees before Boreas, the wintry North Wind, arrived.

Pan

A goat-legged countryside god. Pan looked after shepherds and their flocks, and hung around with *nymphs*. He was also a skilled musician, who played a wind instrument we now call 'pan pipes'.

River gods

Sons of the titans, *Oceanus* and *Tethys*, and the fathers of many of the water nymphs known as *naiads*. One of the river gods was the father of *Daphne*, and he used his powers to turn her into a tree.

Satyrs

Wild and hairy nature spirits. They followed the god *Dionysus* and loved drinking, dancing and chasing beautiful woodland *nymphs* (whether the *nymphs* were interested or not).

Silenus

The father of all the *satyrs*. He brought up *Zeus's* son *Dionysus* and taught him everything he knew about wine and partying. Later, Silenus rode around behind his foster son on a donkey. Walking was far too much effort for this pleasure-loving old fellow.

Nymphs

Female spirits who looked after a particular type of natural place.
There are lots of types of nymph, such as:

Oreads

Nymphs of mountains
and hilly forests.

Dryads

The gods punished mortals who cut down trees without asking the dryads.

Nymphs of trees and forests.

Hamadryads

Wood nymphs, each connected
to a particular tree. They died
if their tree was cut down.

Naiads

Freshwater nymphs.

Oceanids

Particular naiads, who were
daughters of the titan *Oceanus*.

Nereids

Sea nymphs who lived in the
Aegean (Mediterranean) Sea.

They often accompanied Poseidon and sometimes helped out sailors in trouble.

Daphne

A *naiad nymph*. The god *Apollo* fell madly in love with her and
chased after her. She cried out to her river god father to rescue her,
so he transformed her into a laurel tree to keep her safe.

Echo

An *oread nymph*. She chattered so much that the goddess *Hera*
cursed her. After that, she could only ever repeat what other
people said. She fell in love with *Narcissus*, but was rejected
by him, and slowly faded until she was nothing but an echo.

Thetis

Queen of the *nereid nymphs*. There was a prophecy that said
her son would be greater than his father, so *Zeus* made sure
she married a human, named *Peleus,* so their son wouldn't be
dangerously powerful. That son turned out to be the demigod
hero *Achilles*, so he was still very impressive.

Dryad

Witches, hags and goddesses

Some female spirits had great powers over the lives of humans — and their deaths. Some were helpful, some brought down death and danger, while others simply loved to meddle.

Graeae

Graeae

Three wrinkled hags. They only had one eye which they shared. The hero *Perseus* stole it, leaving them blind, until they'd told him where to find their sister, *Medusa*.

Hecate

A goddess of witchcraft, ghosts and all things magical. Witches called on her to aid them in their spellcasting.

Circe

Circe the sorceress changed Odysseus's friends into pigs by feeding them enchanted food.

A beautiful sorceress, daughter of *Helios* and sister of *Pasiphae*. One of her many powers was the ability to transform any humans who offended her into animals. The hero, *Odysseus*, managed to protect himself from Circe's sorcery by eating the flower of a magical plant.

The Furies

Three angry sisters whose job it was to punish wicked people.
Born out of blood that fell from *Uranus* when his son, *Cronus*, killed
him, they were particularly hard on people who killed their parents.

The Fates

Three female spirits in charge of how long every person would live.
These sisters, who showed no mercy, each had a different job:

Clotho
The spirit who
spun the thread
of life.

Lachesis
Measured out how
much life to give
each person.

Atropos
Cut each person's
thread when their
time was up.

The Fates

The Graces

Three goddesses of lovely things. They were usually seen holding
hands and wearing floaty clothing.

Aglaea
The grace of beauty

Eurynome
The grace of mirth

Thalia
The grace of
cheerfulness

The Graces

The Muses

Nine daughters of *Zeus*. Each was responsible for inspiring humans
to create different forms of art.

Calliope
Epic (long) poetry

Euphrosyne
Dance

Euterpe
Music

Erato
Love poetry

Thalia
Comedy

Polyhymnia
Religious music

Clio
History

Melpomene
Tragedy

*Easily confused with the
Grace of the same name!*

Urania
Astronomy

Monster fighters

The mythical world was full of hideous monsters. Luckily, there were many brave heroes, too, who battled these beasts and (usually) won.

Heracles

Heracles

A demigod – that is, half human and half god – whose father was *Zeus*. Heracles was superhumanly strong and performed many impressive feats. He's famous for completing twelve daunting tasks, including slaying the many-headed *hydra*. (He also sailed with *Jason* on the *Argo*.)

Theseus

An Athenian hero who killed the *minotaur* in Crete. This saved the lives of many young Athenians who were being fed to the beast. But sailing home, disaster struck. He forgot to change his ship's sails from black to white to signal to his father, *Aegeus*, that he was alive. Because of this, *Aegeus* killed himself. Theseus was not a thoughtful type. He was just as bad as a boyfriend and husband, abandoning most of the women who loved him.

Bellerophon

A demigod hero who killed the monstrous *chimera*, with the help of a winged horse named *Pegasus*.

Perseus

The hair of Medusa was made from hissing, coiling snakes.

A demigod, son of *Zeus*. He slew *Medusa*, the snake-haired gorgon, rescued the princess *Andromeda* from a sea monster, and then married her. On a less heroic note, he accidentally killed his grandfather. But as this had been prophesied, he had no chance of avoiding it.

Heroic women

Someone once said that well-behaved women seldom make history. They did not say it about these women.

The Amazons

A fierce tribe of warrior women, descended from the war god *Ares* and a *naiad*. They didn't (usually) marry, and most of them didn't have any use for men, except when they wanted to have babies. The men were quickly dismissed afterwards and didn't get to play any part whatsoever in raising their children.

Hippolyta

Queen of the Amazons. The hero *Heracles* had to get his hands on her belt as one of his tasks. It goes to show how tough she was, as this was supposed to be as difficult a task as killing an invulnerable lion.

Atalanta

A wild huntress. As a baby, she was left in the woods to die, but was saved by a bear and then raised by hunters. Atalanta could outrun and out-hunt almost anyone and had many adventures, from hunting the mighty Calydonian boar, to sailing with *Jason* as one of the *Argonauts*. She ended up being turned into a lion after offending *Aphrodite*.

Atalanta only ever lost one race, when she was distracted into picking up golden apples that were dropped in her path.

Heroes of the Trojan War

When the Trojan prince *Paris* stole King *Menelaus*'s wife, *Helen*, the Greeks declared war on the Trojans. Battles raged for ten years, with huge losses on both sides. But, in the end, the Greeks were victorious.

The Greeks

Menelaus
King of Sparta. Despite the trouble she caused, Menelaus took *Helen* back after the war.

Agamemnon
King of Myceanae, brother of *Menelaus* and the Greek commander.

Odysseus
King of Ithaca. He came up with the plan to sneak the Greek army into Troy inside a wooden horse. But he also had many adventures on his ten-year long voyage home from the war.

Achilles
Demigod hero. His mother, *Thetis*, tried to make it impossible to harm him. But his human father, *Peleus*, stopped her from finishing the job, leaving him with one weak spot: his heel. Unfortunately, it was on exactly this spot that he received a fatal wound from *Paris*.

Patroclus
Achilles's best friend, killed by *Hector*.

Sinon
Persuaded the Trojans to take the soldier-filled horse into their city.

Odysseus

On his travels, Odysseus tied himself to the mast of his ship so he could hear the sirens' song without being lured by them.

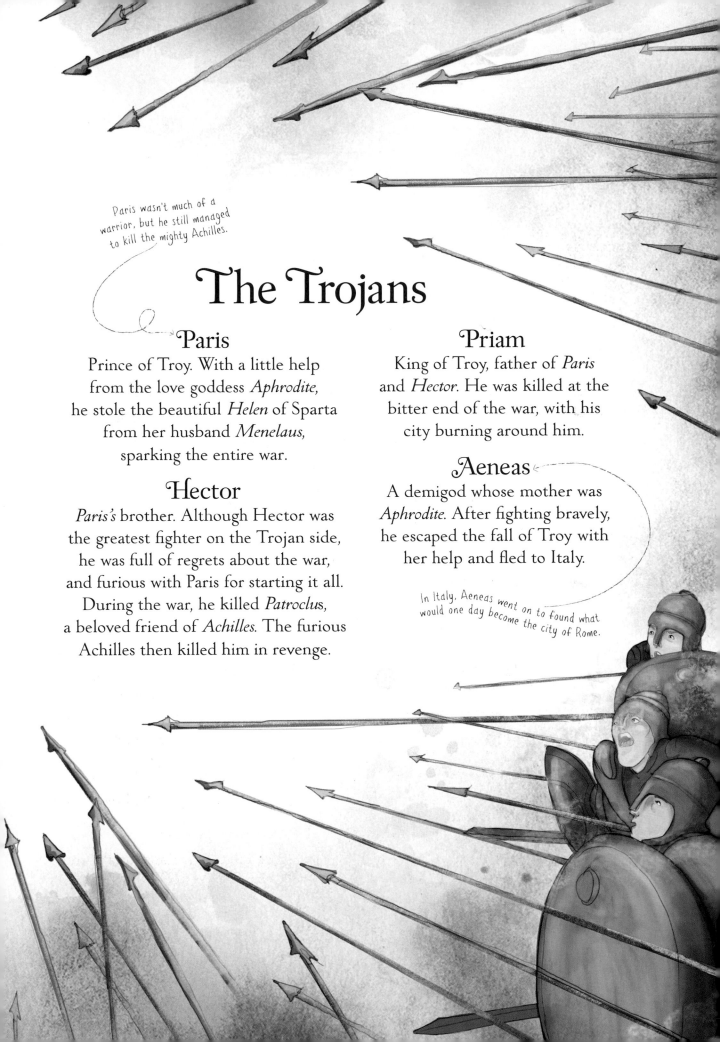

Paris wasn't much of a warrior, but he still managed to kill the mighty Achilles.

The Trojans

Paris

Prince of Troy. With a little help from the love goddess *Aphrodite*, he stole the beautiful *Helen* of Sparta from her husband *Menelaus*, sparking the entire war.

Hector

Paris's brother. Although Hector was the greatest fighter on the Trojan side, he was full of regrets about the war, and furious with Paris for starting it all. During the war, he killed *Patroclus*, a beloved friend of *Achilles*. The furious Achilles then killed him in revenge.

Priam

King of Troy, father of *Paris* and *Hector*. He was killed at the bitter end of the war, with his city burning around him.

Aeneas

A demigod whose mother was *Aphrodite*. After fighting bravely, he escaped the fall of Troy with her help and fled to Italy.

In Italy, Aeneas went on to found what would one day become the city of Rome.

Jason and the Argonauts

One of the most famous of the Greek Myths is *Jason's* quest for the golden fleece. He sailed with a brave band of warriors on a ship named the *Argo*. They became known as the Argonauts, although many of them were also heroes in their own right.

Jason

Rightful King of Iolcus and captain of the *Argo*. His uncle Pelias promised to make Jason king if he brought back the golden fleece from Colchis. (Pelias thought Jason didn't stand a chance of returning in one piece.) But, with *Medea's* help, Jason succeeded, although he never did become king.

Medea

The sorceress *Circe's* niece, and a powerful witch herself. Medea fell in love with *Jason* and used her magic to help his quest succeed. But, later, he left her and she went on a killing spree, murdering his new wife and her own sons, too.

Zetes and Calais

Winged twin sons of Zephyrus, one of the *wind gods*. During the quest, they rescued a king named *Phineas* who was under attack from the evil *harpies*. The twins were later killed by *Heracles*. It was a revenge killing – at one point on the quest for the fleece, a young Argonaut named Hylas went missing. *Heracles*, who was passionately fond of Hylas, went to look for him, and Zetes and Calais persuaded the other Argonauts to leave *Heracles* behind. *Heracles* never forgave them.

Zetes

Calais

The Argonauts

Acastus	Hylas	Palaemon
Admetus	Idas	Palaimonius
Aethalides	Idmon	Peleus
Amphion	Iolaus	Philoctetes
Ancaeus	Iphitos	Phrontis
Argus	Jason	Poeas
Ascalaphus	Laertes	Polydeuces
Atalanta	Laocoon	Polyphemos
Autolycus	Lynceus	Poriclymenus
Bellerophon	Medea	Talaus
Butes	Melas	Telamon
Calais	Meleager	Theseus
Canthus	Mopsus	Tiphys
Castor	Nestor	Zetes
Cytissorus	Oileus	
Echion	Orpheus	
Erginus		
Euphemus		
Euryalus		
Heracles		

Telamon was a close friend of Heracles and went with him to fetch the belt of Hippolyta.

She sailed home with them.

Heracles never found his beloved Hylas, as the boy was captured by nymphs.

Royalty

Whether they were killing a parent or being sacrificed to a sea monster, there was never a dull moment in the lives of these ancient royals.

Pasiphae

Queen of Crete. She was cursed by *Poseidon*, who made her fall in love with a bull. Unsurprisingly, the relationship didn't work out, but the queen gave birth to a half-human, half-bull monster, known as the *minotaur*, as a result.

Minos

King of Crete. He ordered the inventor *Daedalus* to build a fiendishly complicated underground maze, called a labyrinth, to imprison the *minotaur*. Minos then fed young Athenians to the monster, until the hero *Theseus* entered the labyrinth and killed the creature.

Ariadne

Daughter of King *Minos*. Ariadne helped *Theseus* to escape from the labyrinth. She ran away with him, but he abandoned her on an island before he even got home. Ariadne had quite a fun time in the end: the god *Dionysus* fell in love with her while she was sleeping under a tree. He rescued her, and they got married.

Oedipus

King of Thebes. Oedipus was abandoned as a baby when it was predicted that he would kill his father and marry his mother. Unfortunately, his fate was inescapable. The prophecy came true, and when he discovered the awful truth, Oedipus blinded himself as a punishment.

Ariadne

Oedipus

Midas

King of Phrygia. When he was given the power to turn everything he touched to gold, he was thrilled, until he turned his loved ones into statues, and realized he couldn't eat, as his food turned to gold too. He got rid of his power, but later offended *Apollo* and was cursed by having his ears turned to donkey's ears so everyone could see he was a fool.

Midas quickly grew tired of his power to turn things into gold and left his wealthy kingdom behind to live in the woods without a single belonging.

Clytemnestra

Queen of Myceanae, wife of *Agamemnon* and half sister of *Helen*. Her marriage was not a happy one. *Agamemnon* was having an affair with *Cassandra*, a Trojan princess who had prophetic visions. Meanwhile, Clytemnestra had a boyfriend of her own. It all ended in a bloodbath, when Clytemnestra's boyfriend murdered *Agamemnon*, and she killed *Cassandra*.

Aegeus

King of Athens and father of *Theseus* (by magic). After believing that his son was dead, grief-stricken Aegeus threw himself into the sea and drowned. This sea was later named the Aegean after him.

Andromeda

Princess of Ethiopia. Her parents insulted the god *Poseidon* so they had to sacrifice her to a sea monster to calm him down. But while she was chained to a rock waiting to be eaten, *Perseus* swooped down on his winged sandals and rescued her.

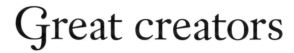

Great creators

These people were some of the most skilled mortals in the ancient lands. Sometimes their abilities brought them happiness, but for others, they were a curse.

Daedalus

Daedalus

Inventor and all-round genius. Daedalus created a labyrinth for King *Minos* and designed working wings for himself and his son, *Icarus*. This was out of necessity, not just for fun: *Minos* had imprisoned the two of them in a tower and it was their only hope of escape.

Penelope

Faithful wife of *Odysseus*. Her husband was away from home for so long that other men pestered her to remarry. She said she'd choose one of them when she'd finished a burial cloth she was weaving for *Odysseus's* elderly father. Then she sneakily unpicked a little of it each night so she never had to keep her promise.

Arachne

A very talented weaver. But Arachne was foolish enough to claim she was even better at weaving than the goddess *Athena*. Whether or not it was true, *Athena* punished her for speaking out by turning her into a spider. The reason that spiders are all so good at weaving webs is because they're descended from Arachne.

Pygmalion

Pygmalion

King of Cyprus, and a sculptor. Pygmalion couldn't find true love, so he made himself a statue of his ideal woman, then fell in love with it. The goddess *Aphrodite* brought the statue to life and they lived happily ever after.

286

Beautiful people

The good looks of some characters in the Greek Myths caused no end of trouble. One young man was so handsome he fell for himself, while another girl was so lovely that she sparked the Trojan War.

Adonis

Had affairs with both *Persephone* and *Aphrodite*. He was killed by jealous *Ares*, who disguised himself as a boar and attacked him. Anemone flowers sprang up where Adonis's blood fell.

Ganymede

A boy so beautiful, he caught the eye of *Zeus* who turned into an eagle and carried him to *Olympus* to serve the gods.

Narcissus

A pretty boy, but not that bright. He fell in love with his own reflection, ignoring the love of a *nymph* named *Echo*. In the end, he turned into a flower, which became known as a narcissus.

Helen

The beautiful daughter of *Zeus* and a woman named Leda. The Trojan War began after *Paris* stole Helen from her Greek husband, *Menelaus*. She became known as the "face that launched a thousand ships" – war ships, that is.

Psyche

Lover of *Eros*. He visited her under cover of darkness and wouldn't let her look at him. When she disobeyed, he left her. But she won him back in the end and *Zeus* made her immortal.

Ill~fated people

Life in Greek Myths was never easy, but some people had an especially tough time, either through their own fault, or because they irritated the wrong god.

Pandora

The one good thing to come out of Pandora's terrible box was the spirit of hope.

A woman made by the gods and given to the *titan Epimetheus* to be his wife. *Zeus* made her full of curiosity, and then gave her a box that she wasn't allowed to open. Predictably, she opened it, and let loose every bad thing in the world.

Cassandra

A Trojan princess, sister of *Paris* and *Hector. Apollo* loved her, and gave her the ability to see the future. But she didn't love him back, so he made sure no one believed her visions. As a result, she couldn't persuade the Trojans not to go to war with the Greeks, even though she knew they were certain to lose.

Cassandra

Icarus

The foolish son of clever *Daedalus*. Wearing his father's homemade wings, he flew higher than he should, and went too close to the sun. The wax on his wings melted, and he fell to his death.

Phineas

King of Thrace. He could see the future, but the gods didn't take kindly to him sharing his visions with others. So they blinded him and sent the cruel *harpies* to torture him. He was eventually rescued by the Argonauts, *Zetes* and *Calais*.

Orpheus

Best musician on earth. He's most famous for his mission to the *Underworld* to bring his wife back from the dead. Sadly, he failed at the last minute and lost her forever.

Tantalus

A son of *Zeus*. He offended the gods by serving them a disgusting meal of his own dead son and was doomed to starve for eternity, with delicious fruit just out of his reach.

Sisyphus

Grandfather of *Bellerophon*. After offending *Zeus* and *Hades*, he was made to push a boulder up a hill for eternity. Every time he reached the top, the boulder rolled down again.

Phaithon

Son of *Helios*. He persuaded his father to let him drive the blazing chariot that carried the sun. But he wasn't a good driver and scorched the earth, so *Zeus* killed him.

Peleus

Father of *Achilles*. He invited gods and spirits to his wedding, but forgot spiteful *Eris*, who stirred up trouble in *Olympus*. This prompted *Aphrodite* to help *Paris* steal *Helen*, which, in turn, sparked the Trojan War.

Sisyphus

Strange creatures

Some characters in the myths were mixtures of several different kinds of beasts, while others were animals with amazing abilities. Some of the strangest were mixtures of human and animal parts.

Minotaur

A man-eating monster with a man's body and the head of a bull. The minotaur was the product of an unlikely love affair between *Pasiphae*, the queen of Crete, and a bull. This monster lived in the labyrinth on Crete, enjoying regular feasts on human flesh, until it was killed by *Theseus*.

Centaurs

Human above the waist but all horse below that. Centaurs were hunters and fighters who usually lived in forests. Some of them were rough and tough, others were highly educated.

Cheiron

Cheiron

The oldest and wisest of the centaurs. Cheiron was an excellent teacher of everything from music to hunting. He was immortal in theory, but chose to die after *Heracles* accidentally wounded him.

The minotaur was a unique creature, the only one of his species. But one of him was bad enough and he butchered countless innocent young men and women before he was killed.

Pegasus

A pure white, immortal flying horse, who sprang from the neck of *Medusa* when *Perseus* hacked off her head. Helped the hero *Bellerophon* defeat the dreadful *chimera*. In the end, he flew up to live on *Olympus*, where he pulled *Zeus's* chariot.

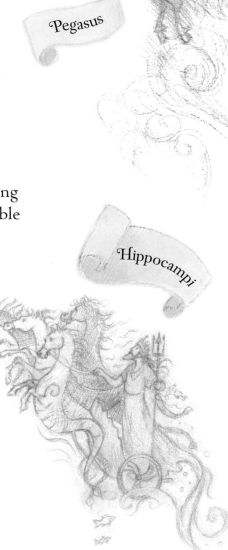

Pegasus

Nemean lion

A lion with such tough skin that it couldn't be harmed by any weapon. *Heracles* got around this by strangling it with his bare hands. Then he wore its skin as a protective cloak.

Ceryneian stag

A speedy, golden-horned stag that belonged to the hunting goddess *Artemis*. It was so fast that it was almost impossible to catch. Even the mighty *Heracles* had to chase it for an entire year before he eventually caught it.

Hippocampi

Hippocampi

These creatures looked like horses from the front, but had fishlike tails, and scales all over their bodies. They pulled the god *Poseidon's* chariot through the seas, and *nereid nymphs* rode them like ponies.

Griffins

Winged beasts with eagles' heads and wings, and lions' bodies. Griffins often guarded treasure.

291

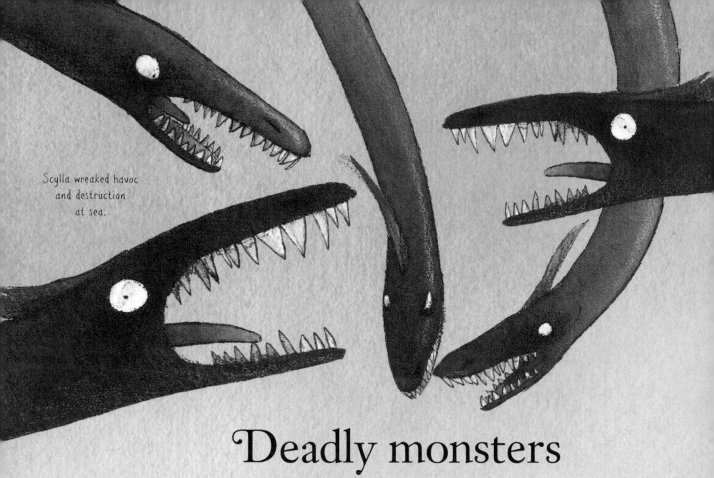

Scylla wreaked havoc and destruction at sea.

Deadly monsters

Monsters were everywhere. Heroes were never safe from their gnashing jaws and slicing claws.

Charybdis

Not exactly a monster, but an enormous whirlpool that wrecked countless ships and caused many sailors to drown.

Scylla

A gigantic evil sea monster with six snake-like heads and a ring of snarling dogs around her waist. Scylla was always found close to *Charybdis*, and *Odysseus* had to navigate these perilous twin obstacles on his voyage home.

Cerberus

Cerberus

A three-headed dog with a dragon's tail. It guarded the entrance to the *Underworld*. Cerberus was fierce, but could be distracted by beautiful music or tasty (drugged) food.

Hydra

A monster with many heads. When one head was cut off, two grew in its place. The hydra lived in a swamp near Lerna. It was killed by *Heracles* as one of his tasks.

Harpies

Screeching winged female monsters with strong talons. Best known for tormenting *Phineas* by snatching his food.

Medusa the Gorgon

A monster with snakes for hair. Looking at her hideous face turned people to stone. But *Perseus* killed her by peering at her reflection in his shield as they fought.

Polyphemus

A cyclops who was a son of *Poseidon*. He was blinded in his one eye by *Odysseus*, who then stole his sheep.

Sirens

Like *harpies*, sirens were half bird, half woman. They sang songs to lure sailors onto jagged rocks in choppy seas.

Sphinx

Had the body of a lion, the breast and head of a woman, an eagle's wings and a snaky tail. She terrorized Thebes, eating anyone who couldn't answer a riddle she told. She was defeated when *Oedipus* answered correctly.

Chimera

A monster that was part lion, part goat, part snake. This mixed-up monster was killed by the hero *Bellerophon*.

Otherworldly places

The Greek Myths are set in a world that's not unlike our own, but the stories also take you to some very strange and magical places.

Olympus

Palace of the gods. It was built in the clouds, high above a mountain, which later became known as Mount Olympus. Occasionally a mortal would be brought to live there with the gods, but usually as a servant rather than just to enjoy themselves. The gods who lived there (*Zeus, Hera, Poseidon, Demeter, Ares, Hermes, Hephaestus, Aphrodite, Athena, Apollo, Artemis* and *Hestia*) became known as the Olympian gods.

Ocean

A great body of water that encircled the earth. The ocean was ruled by the god *Poseidon*, who lived there along with various water *nymphs* and sea monsters.

Earth

Similar to the world we know, except that gods walked among humans and monsters lurked around every corner. The earth was flat according to most Ancient Greeks. (You'll find maps of lots of places from the Greek Myths on pages 297-299.)

Charon and the River Styx

Charon was the ferryman of the River Styx,
a wide, underground river that marked the boundary
between the *earth* and the *Underworld*. To cross to the *Underworld*,
you had to pay Charon a silver coin called an obol. Any dead souls
who couldn't pay would spend eternity drifting between the lands
of the living and the dead.

The Underworld

Ruled by the god *Hades* and his queen *Persephone*, this vast kingdom
beneath the *earth* was where the souls of the dead went when they died.
The gates of the Underworld were guarded by a monstrous dog named
Cerberus. Once they were through the gates, the dead were sent to
one of three main areas:

Elysian Fields

The VIP lounge of the Underworld, reserved for particularly good
or heroic people or those loved by the gods. This was a gorgeous,
leafy pleasure garden.

Asphodel Fields

Most ordinary mortals went here and led drab afterlives in this
shadowy place. However, heroes who died in battle could be sent
here too. They had to spend eternity surrounded by the puny,
wittering spirits of nobodies, which doesn't seem very fair.

Tartarus

Evildoers ended up in this part of the Underworld.
It was a dark pit, where souls suffered eternal tortures,
often designed for the individual by *Zeus* himself.

The souls of the dead were shadowy versions
of their former selves, known as shades.

295

Where did it all happen?

On these maps, you can find all kinds of gods, monsters and heroes, follow their adventures and locate lots of the places mentioned in the stories.

The Greek Myths were written down over a thousand years ago, long before the region was divided into countries as it is today. In those days, it was made up of lots of small states or kingdoms. These are shown in capital letters.

Ancient Greece

VIII
The king of Thrace kept his man-eating horses here.

THRACE

MACEDONIA

The Greek gods lived in a palace, called Olympus, high in the clouds above a mountain.

CHALCIDICE

IX
Heracles went this way to bring back the Amazon queen's belt.

DARDANIA

Mount Olympus

ILLYRIA

PIERIA

•Troy

Lemnos

The Greeks used a giant wooden horse to win the war against the Trojans.

THESSALY

This is where Cheiron taught Achilles how to fight.

Lesbos

Iolcus• ▲Mount Pelion

PHTHIA MALIS

Theseus was pushed off a cliff to his death on Scyros.

Scyros

AEGEAN SEA

DORIS

EUBOEA

AETOLIA

III
Golden-horned stag

IV
Wild boar

Chios

Narcissas

I
Nemean lion

PHOCIS
•Delphi

BOEOTIA

Bellerophon found Pegasus here.

This is where Icarus fell to his death.

Ithaca

LOCRIS

ACHAEA

ATTICA

Mount Erymanthos ▲

Corinth

•Athens

ICARIAN SEA

Nemea

ELIS

ARCADIA

•Stymphalis

Argos• •Tiryns

Theseus became King of Athens.

V
King Augeas of Elis had his stinking stables here.

Lerna

PELOPONNESE

ARGOLID

King Eurystheus's palace was at Tiryns.

Seriphos

Naxos

II
The hydra lived in a swamp near Lerna.

Dionysus fell in love with Ariadne on Naxos.

MESSENIA

Sparta•

LACONIA

Perseus grew up among fishermen on the island of Seriphos.

This is where Theseus slew the minotaur.

VI
Heracles shot down a flock of birds that was plaguing Stymphalis.

•Cape Taenarum

IONIAN SEA

XII
Heracles entered the Underworld here to capture Cerberus.

VII
Heracles took the Cretan bull from King Minos's palace at Knossos.

X and XI
Heracles went this way to bring back Geryon's red cattle and three golden apples from the garden of the Hesperides.

CRETE

•Knossos

I~XII Heracles's tasks

Ancient Greece and the Mediterranean

This is where Phaithon crashed to earth, after losing control of the chariot of the sun.

ALPS

River Po

ADRIATIC SEA

This is where Circe the sorceress turned Odysseus's men into pigs.

CORSICA

MEDITERRANEAN SEA

Sirens lured sailors to the rocks with their song here.

The King of the Winds had his palace here.

SARDINIA

Atlas was turned to stone here, when Perseus showed him Medusa's head.

Poseidon ruled the seas.

This is where the cyclops lived in his cave.

SICILY

This is where Helios grazed his immortal sheep and cows.

GARDEN OF THE HESPERIDES

ATLAS MOUNTAINS

Odysseus and his men stopped off here before their encounter with the cyclops.

LIBYA

There have been snakes in the Libyan Desert ever since Perseus spilled the Medusa's blood there as he flew over.

LIBYAN DESERT

Medea helped Jason to take the golden fleece from here.

COLCHIS

BLACK SEA

Jason and the Argonauts probably took this route home to avoid having to sail the stormy seas and pass the sirens again.

After the Argonauts made it through the Clashing Rocks, the rocks stopped moving forever.

River Danube

Blind King Phineus lived here under the constant watch of the harpies.

Achilles was mortally wounded at Troy.

King Midas washed off his golden touch in a river here.

The Amazons lived in a land on the shores of the Black Sea.

THRACE

MACEDONIA

PHRYGIA

Troy

Sardis

Jason was the rightful King of Iolcus.

Odysseus was King of Ithaca.

Iolcus

SYRIA

River Pactolus

LYCIA

Delphi

Thebes

Athens

IONIAN SEA

Mycenae

ITHACA

Sparta

CYPRUS

PHOENICIA

Helen was Queen of Sparta before she was taken to Troy.

The Chimera lived here.

Scylla and Charybdis

CRETE

MEDITERRANEAN SEA

Alexandria

Cairo

EGYPT

River Nile

Jason's voyage
Odysseus's voyage

Glossary

This word list defines some of the words you may come across while reading about the Greek Myths.

Amazon
A member of a tribe of strong, tall warrior women who are said to have lived near the Black Sea.

Argonaut
A sailor on the ship, the *Argo*.

Centaur
A magical creature. Half horse, half man.

Chariot
A wheeled vehicle, usually pulled by horses.

Constellation
A cluster of stars. Many are named after Greek characters.

Cretan
Someone or something that comes from the island of Crete.

Curse
Magic spell that brings bad luck.

Cyclops
A giant being with only one eye.

Demigod
Usually the child of a god and a human.

Eternity
Lasting forever and ever.

Fate
An inescapable power that controls events in a person's life. Decided by three goddesses called the Fates.

God
An immortal being with special powers.

Gorgon
A monstrous woman with snakes for hair.

Harpy
A vicious monster. Half woman, half bird of prey.

Hero
A particularly brave, strong or clever human being or demigod.

Immortal
A being that can live forever.

Labyrinth
A maze built on Crete to imprison the minotaur.

Lyre
A musical instrument, similar to a harp.

Minotaur
A man-eating monster. Half human, half bull.

Mortal
A being, generally a human, that can die.

Myth
An ancient story that attempts to explain the origins of a group of people.

Nymph
A female spirit connected to part of the natural world.

Obol
A silver coin. The Ancient Greeks buried the dead with an obol to pay their way to the Underworld.

Olympian
A being, usually a god, that lives in Olympus.

Oracle
A message from the gods, often told by a priestess.

Prophecy
A vision of the future.

Sacrifice
A gift offered to the gods to ask for good treatment.

Satyr
A nature spirit, a hairy man, often with a tail and donkeys' ears.

Shade
The shadowy, ghost-like version of a person that goes to the Underworld after he or she dies.

Siren
A monster that lures sailors onto jagged rocks with enchanting songs. Half woman, half bird.

Spartan
A person or thing that comes from Sparta.

Temple
A building where gods are worshipped and sacrifices are offered to them.

Titan
A giant.

Trojan
A person or thing that comes from the city of Troy.

Underworld
The land of the dead. Ruled by the god Hades.

Wreath
A crown of intertwined leaves.

Greek and Roman names

After the Ancient Greeks, another group of people, the Romans, became very powerful in the Mediterranean region. They adopted many of the Greek gods as their own and sometimes changed their names. Here you can see the Greek names followed by the different Roman ones.

Aphrodite/Venus
Artemis/Diana
Ares/Mars
Athena/Minerva
Cronus/Saturn
Demeter/Ceres
Dionysus/Bacchus
Eros/Cupid

Gaia/Tellus
Hades/Dis *or* Pluto
Hebe/Juventas
Hecate/Hecate
Hephaestus/Vulcan
Hera/Juno
Heracles/Hercules
Hermes/Mercury

Hestia/Vesta
Nyx/Nox
Persephone/Proserpine
Poseidon/Neptune
Rhea/Ops
Uranus/Caelus
Zeus/Jupiter

Index

Digital design by John Russell; Additional editorial contribution by Conrad Mason

When using the internet please follow the internet safety guidelines displayed on the Usborne Quicklinks Website.
Usborne Publishing Ltd. is not responsible for the content or availability of any website other than its own.
We recommend that children are supervised while using the internet.